o, Jade.
In."

"Yo   houghtful,
up-a   ld work on
your people skills, J.T. They were never your strong
point."

"Oh, that's good, coming from you."

She flicked him a warning look, but Jeremy knew
the palace gates were strong enough to hold off a
tank, so they'd probably be able to protect him
from a single reporter.

Even Jade.

"Besides, my people skills are fine, babe," he
assured her. "It's my 'reporter' skills you seem to
be having trouble with. And frankly, if you don't
like 'em, then I must be doing something right."

"As charming as ever, I see," Jade retorted.

"You used to think I was pretty damn charming."

"I used to believe in Santa Claus, too."

Dear Reader,

This season of harvest brings a cornucopia of six new passionate, powerful and provocative love stories from Silhouette Desire for your enjoyment.

Don't miss our current MAN OF THE MONTH title, Cindy Gerard's *Taming the Outlaw,* a reunion romance featuring a cowboy dealing with the unexpected consequences of a hometown summer of passion. And of course you'll want to read Katherine Garbera's *Cinderella's Convenient Husband,* the tenth absorbing title in Silhouette Desire's DYNASTIES: THE CONNELLYS continuity series.

A Navy SEAL is on a mission to win the love of the woman he left behind, in *The SEAL's Surprise Baby* by Amy J. Fetzer, while a TV anchorwoman gets up close and personal with a high-ranking soldier in *The Royal Treatment* by Maureen Child. This is the latest title in the exciting Silhouette crossline series CROWN AND GLORY.

Opposites attract when a sexy hunk and a matchmaker share digs in *Hearts Are Wild* by Laura Wright. And in *Secrets, Lies and...Passion* by Linda Conrad, a single mom is drawn into a web of desire and danger by the lover who jilted her at the altar years before...or did he?

Experience all six of these sensuous romances from Silhouette Desire this month, and guarantee that your Halloween will be all treat, no trick.

Enjoy!

Joan Marlow Golan

Joan Marlow Golan
Senior Editor, Silhouette Desire

Please address questions and book requests to:
Silhouette Reader Service
U.S.: 3010 Walden Ave., P.O. Box 1325, Buffalo, NY 14269
Canadian: P.O. Box 609, Fort Erie, Ont. L2A 5X3

The Royal Treatment

MAUREEN CHILD

Published by Silhouette Books

America's Publisher of Contemporary Romance

Special thanks and acknowledgment are given to Maureen Child for her contribution to the CROWN AND GLORY series.

 SILHOUETTE BOOKS

ISBN 0-373-76468-5

THE ROYAL TREATMENT

Visit Silhouette at www.eHarlequin.com

Printed in U.S.A.

MAUREEN CHILD

is a California native who loves to travel. Every chance they get, she and her husband are taking off on another research trip. The author of more than sixty books, Maureen loves a happy ending and still swears that she has the best job in the world. She lives in Southern California with her husband, two children and a golden retriever with delusions of grandeur.

Visit her Web site at www.maureenchild.com.

To everyone at the A.S.P.E.N. in Galveston conference.
It was a memorable week—you guys are the best.

One

———

Jeremy Wainwright checked his wristwatch, then lifted his gaze to sweep the exterior of the palace. The three-story structure looked like something out of a fairy tale. The gray limestone seemed to shimmer in the crisp, clear November air, and late afternoon sunlight dazzled the gleaming, mullioned window panes. He had a feeling that if he listened just right, he'd be able to hear the clang of long-silent swords and the proud blast of trumpets.

He felt a strong connection to this place and its history. For more than two hundred years, the Wainwrights had been here, on Penwyck, protecting the royal family, guarding the palace. They'd served with pride and honor, every last one of them, and he was proud to take his place among them.

The wind off the sea had a bite to it and made Jeremy grateful for the thick blue sweater he wore. The trees in the courtyard and those just outside the palace walls bore the bright stamp of autumn. Red, gold, yellow leaves rustled in the wind and floated down to litter the palace yard with bits of color.

But Jeremy didn't take time to appreciate the beauty of the place. Instead, his sharp-eyed gaze, alert for trouble, continued a thorough yet quick scan, noting that everything seemed to be as it should be. The Royal Guard walked the perimeter, rifles at their shoulders. The iron scroll-work gates, which had protected the palace for centuries, stood closed, locked, impenetrable. And the last of the tour groups were just leaving the public half of the palace.

Good. Jeremy never really relaxed until the gates were closed behind interlopers. Oh, he knew it was important for the citizens of Penwyck—not to mention international visitors—to be able to tour the palace. At least the rooms set aside for public viewing.

But tours were a security man's nightmare.

There were just too many things that could go wrong. One man getting past a checkpoint with a concealed weapon could turn into a hostage drama.

And then there was the headache of a tourist wandering away from the crowd and finding his or her way into the royal family's apartments. Not to mention the queen's habit of sometimes surprising the tours with a royal visit.

Shaking his head, Jeremy kept an eye on the chattering visitors leaving through the iron gates, and didn't stop watching until those gates were sealed again. Once they had been, he stepped into the tiny guard station to pour himself an end-of-shift cup of coffee.

Taking a sip of the strong, black liquid, he let the heat of it roll through him, and ignored the raised voices filtering to him from the gates. Whoever it was, his guards could handle it. Picked as the best of the best from the Royal Army, and trained by him, they could handle anything. Their duty was to protect the king and queen and the rest of the royal family. And there wasn't a one of them that Jeremy didn't trust to lay down his life for the royals.

And by the sound of things, he thought suddenly, that might just be on today's agenda. Setting his coffee cup down on the desk, he stepped out of the kiosk and listened more carefully to the raised voices.

"Damn it," Jeremy muttered. "Trouble couldn't wait five more minutes?" He checked that his pistol was discreetly tucked on his right hip, beneath the bulk of his sweater, and then headed for the gate.

Naturally, he heard the woman first. Not difficult, since she made no attempt to keep her voice down. He stopped midstep as he recognized that voice. It hit him hard. Just as it did every damn time he dreamed about her.

Jade Erickson.

Lover.

Ex-wife.

Pain in the neck.

"Not too late," he muttered. "Still time to get in your car and let the next poor fool on duty handle her." His shift was over. Let Lieutenant Gimble take care of this. "Hell," Jeremy grumbled with a disgusted snort, "that's like sending a kid with a peashooter up against an armed tank."

He just couldn't do it to Gimble.

Penwyck was too damn small, that's what the problem was. For three years, he'd managed to avoid a face-to-face confrontation with the woman he'd once promised to love, honor and cherish forever. But he saw plenty of her anyway. Every time he turned on the news.

Jade Erickson was PEN-TV's latest darling. Once upon a time, she'd been *his* darling. But those days, he reminded himself, were long gone.

She stood five-foot-five, and packed a lot of

curves onto that tiny frame. Curves he remembered all too well. Her shoulder-length auburn hair danced about her face in the sharp, cold wind. He could still recall the feel of that silken mass sliding across his skin, and his fingers itched to touch it again. In memory, he saw her sea-green eyes go smoky and soft with pleasure as he loved her. Now those eyes were narrowed and shooting daggers at the lieutenant.

Thinner than he remembered, she wore a black suit that clung to every curve, a white blouse and a diamond that flashed from her left lapel. When they were together, she hadn't had diamonds. Jeremy couldn't afford them. He'd bought her a small aquamarine—the color of her eyes—set in gold for an engagement ring. But that was gone now, too.

Her long fingers were curled around the scrolled emblem on the palace gates, and as he watched, she gave it a good shake. He laughed shortly. She hadn't changed *too* much, then. That temper of hers still simmered just below the surface. She made a helluva picture, and Jeremy was male enough to appreciate it even while already working on ways to get rid of her.

He caught the young soldier's glance and waved him off. "I'll take care of this," he said.

"Yes, sir." The lieutenant beat a hasty—and grateful—retreat.

Jeremy turned to face her then, and his breath actually caught in his throat. Staring into those seafoam-colored eyes of hers he felt like he'd been hit over the head. Damn. She still packed a punch.

He had to force himself to speak after a few seconds of stiff silence. "Jade."

"J.T."

Jeremy Thomas. J.T. Only his family called him that. It sounded good hearing it from her again. Damn it.

She cleared her throat, and he wondered if she'd felt the slam of desire as hard as he had. Then he decided he was better off not knowing.

"What are you doing here, Jade?"

"You know why I'm here."

Yes, he did. Stubborn woman. "If it's about the interview, then you're wasting your time. And more importantly, *mine.*"

"Blast it, J.T.," she said, and gave the gates another shake for good measure. "You should be helping me."

"Why would I do that?" he asked.

"For old times' sake?"

He glanced past her to the skinny, older man standing behind her with a camera perched on his bony shoulder. Lowering his voice, Jeremy shifted his gaze back to her and said, "Old times' sake? Are you nuts?"

She blew out a breath that ruffled the wisps of hair dusting her forehead. "Fine." She let go of the gates and lifted her gaze to glare at him. "No old times. But the least you could do is be civil."

"I was civil," he reminded her, "the first three times you requested this stupid interview."

"I thought if I came down here and we could talk, face-to-face, you'd change your mind."

"Wrong."

"The king is sick, J.T., and the queen—"

"The queen is attending her husband and doesn't want to do an interview."

"She has to say something."

"She will. When *she* decides to."

"I'm just trying to do my job," Jade said.

"So am I."

She tapped the toe of one high-heeled shoe against the pavement. "The people have a right to know."

"The people have a right to know about business. They don't have a right to invade the royal family's private life."

"The king is sick," she argued.

"And being cared for."

"By whom?"

"You know," he said, leaning in closer still, "if you had put half this determination into our marriage…"

She flushed. Good to know she could still do that.

Her cameraman moved closer, a small red light blinking at the base of the lens, and Jeremy lifted one hand, pointing at him. "Turn that thing off."

"Do it, Harry," Jade ordered without even looking at the man. The cameraman complied and moved off a few paces.

When they were alone again, she pushed her hair back out of her face, looked up at him and said, "J.T., I only want five minutes of her time."

"The queen is busy with her husband. She puts a high priority on caring for her family."

Jade winced at the direct hit. "Low blow, J.T."

"Maybe," he acknowledged, and admitted silently that he'd be better off not stirring up old resentments. What good would it do, anyway? "But you're still not getting through the gates."

"This isn't the end of it, you know."

"Yeah, I know."

"This is important to me."

"I can't help you." And that didn't make him as happy as he'd thought it would. She could still get to him. Just being this close to her, inhaling the scent of her flowery perfume, was enough to wipe the years away and take him back to that small apartment they'd shared. Back when they'd thought they had a future.

When they were young and naive.

Back when they'd thought love would be enough.

She looked past him, toward the castle doors and across the grounds, before shifting her gaze back to his. He could see the wheels turning in her brain and knew that she was far from finished with this. He'd never met a more hardheaded woman. Strange to think now that that was one of the first things he'd liked about her.

"So this means war?" she asked, and he recognized the tone. Whenever Jade got scared or felt pushed into a corner, she went stiff and snotty.

"If that's the way you want it," he said. Jeremy hid a smile of appreciation as he watched her fight down a wave of anger that was clearly clawing at her throat. But he had to give her credit. After a few seconds, she'd managed it. She hadn't always been able to put a lid on that temper. He still had the scar on his forehead from when she'd pitched a plate at him.

On their honeymoon, no less.

But along with that scar, he also had the memory of how they'd spent hours making up. It had been well worth that little scar.

Taking a deep breath, she said, "You need to put someone else on this gate. Your little soldier there is a moron."

One dark eyebrow lifted as the desire crouched inside him eased back a bit. "Is he?"

"He refused to let me inside," she snapped. "Refused to even answer my questions."

"Well then," Jeremy told her, "the lieutenant is clearly as bright as I'd thought him to be."

She sighed, tapped her shoe a little harder, then put both hands on those deliciously curved hips.

Jeremy chuckled, folded his arms across his chest and planted his feet wide apart. Comfortable in his fighting stance, he said, "You might as well go, Jade. You're not getting in."

"You know," she said, giving him a thoughtful, up and down look, "you really should work on your people skills, J.T. They never were your strong point."

"Oh, that's good, coming from you. Judging by the conversation you were having with Lieutenant Gimble, you're in no position to give lectures on winning friends and influencing people yourself."

She inhaled sharply and blew the air out in a rush. "All right, I'm sorry about that. I haven't lost my temper in a long time."

He fingered that old scar just above his eyebrow. "That's a shame. Fury does great things for your eyes."

She flicked him a warning look, but Jeremy knew those gates were strong enough to hold off a tank, so they'd probably be able to protect him from a single reporter.

Even Jade.

"Besides, my people skills are fine, babe," he assured her. "It's my 'reporter' skills you seem to be having trouble with. And frankly, if you don't like 'em, then I must be doing something right."

"As charming as ever, I see," Jade retorted.

"You used to think I was pretty damn charming."

"I used to believe in Santa Claus, too," Jade said tightly. "Then I grew up."

Frustration simmered just below the anger surging inside her. Out of all the men on this little island, why did it have to be her ex-husband standing between her and her goal?

She stared up—*way* up—into J.T.'s hard brown eyes and didn't see a glimmer of hope there. She did, however, feel that slow, sweet surge of want rise up inside her again. From the moment she'd locked eyes with him, she'd felt it. A heady rush of pulse-pounding desire that was so thick it nearly choked her. And she sensed he'd felt it, too.

It was as if the last three years hadn't happened. Three long years of not seeing him, not hearing his voice, not feeling his touch, and one look from him and she was going up like a skyrocket.

"Jade?" Her cameraman's voice cut into her thoughts and she sent the tall, thin, older man a quick look. "I'm heading back to the van."

She nodded, and thought she caught a wisp of a

satisfied smirk on J.T.'s face. Irritating, frustrating, completely sexy man.

Once Harry had moved off, she switched her attention back to the wall of muscle that stood between she and her destiny. She'd tried being nice. She'd tried being commanding. Nothing had worked.

"Look," she said, trying yet again, and this time using her patented let's-be-friends tone of voice, "there's no reason we can't come to a meeting of the minds."

A corner of his mouth twitched. She thought. It was there and gone so fast she couldn't really be sure. Still, she latched on to that one small hope and kept talking in the same, gentle tone. "We're adults. We're professionals. Surely there's a way we can solve this...difficulty."

He snorted and unfolded his arms, giving her a lovely view of a chest broad enough to star in dozens of female fantasies. As she knew all too well. "You're really something," he said, his gaze running up and down her body quickly and yet so thoroughly it was almost as if he'd touched her.

She squirmed a bit against the flash of heat that briefly dazzled her bloodstream, but held her ground. She hadn't been intimidated into leaving. She certainly wouldn't be *aroused* into leaving.

"Thank you," she said.

"Wasn't a compliment."

She inhaled sharply, deeply, then dug her manicured nails into her palms as she fisted her hands.

"Jade," he continued, before she could think of something suitably witty to say, "I've told you every day, you're not getting in here. So why don't you do us both a favor and go away?"

"I'm just trying to do my job," she repeated.

"So am I."

"Fine." She could be generous. Find some common ground. "I understand that."

"See," he said, planting his hands on his hips, "I don't think you do."

"Your job is to protect the royal family. But I'm not a threat."

"Not every threat is a physical one."

Jade felt the pulse of anger quicken inside her. "I only want to do an interview with *my* queen."

"And *my* queen," he countered, "isn't interested."

"She can't stay hidden away forever."

"She's the queen. She can pretty much do what she wants."

"This isn't the Middle Ages, you know," Jade snapped, giving in to the fury goading her into a fight with the bane of her existence. "We aren't simple crofters huddled around campfires."

"Too bad," J.T. said. "As I recall, you look

pretty good by firelight." Motioning to Lieutenant Gimble to come closer, he said, "Good seeing you again, Jade."

"This isn't over, J.T."

"Sure it is." Then he flicked her a quick glance. "You've still got great legs, babe."

"You can't walk away from me like—" She broke off. Pointless to keep arguing when the man whose neck you wanted to wring was already striding away from you.

The young lieutenant gave her a wary glance and a wide berth. Jade ignored him and stared after J.T., with a look cold and hard enough that, had he been the slightest bit more sensitive, would have sent him to his knees. As it was, he walked through the double doors to the palace and disappeared.

Disgusted, she gave in to the urge riding her and kicked the iron gate. All she accomplished with that smooth move was to darn near break her foot.

She limped down the drive to the sidewalk and the van waiting for her at the curb. Amazing. Five minutes with J.T. and her professionalism had dissolved into a sea of raging hormones and temper.

Sometimes "ex" didn't really mean a thing, did it?

Two

Jade walked into her apartment, tossed her purse and keys onto the narrow hall table and slammed the door behind her. Automatically, she snapped both locks, then slapped the chain into place. She took extra care in turning the new dead bolt.

Temper, she warned herself, then kicked off her shoes and limped across the room in her stocking feet. Her toes ached. "Darn him, anyway. Why did it have to be *him?* Thousands of soldiers in the army, and J.T.'s the one I have to deal with."

The plush, mauve carpet caressed the soles of her feet as she walked straight across the neat, uncluttered living room to the sliding glass doors. She flipped the lock, pushed the heavy panel open and stepped out onto her balcony.

The wind slapped at her, made her shiver, but she welcomed the cold, hoping it would put out the fire still burning in her blood. But the chances of that were pretty slim. Like it or not, J.T. could do things to her with a look that any other man wouldn't be able to accomplish with a touch.

Jade sighed, reached up and rubbed her eyes with her fingertips, as if by doing so she could wipe away the memory of J.T.'s penetrating gaze. Seeing him again shouldn't have been so hard. Three years had passed. Three long, busy, *lonely* years. It should have been more than enough time to get him out of her mind and heart.

But nothing about her relationship with J.T. had *ever* been easy. Jade closed her eyes and saw his face again. Those dark, chocolate eyes that seemed deep enough to hold the secrets of the universe.

She blew out a long, shaky breath. Her hair flew about her face and she reached up to scoop the long strands back. Tipping her face into the breeze, she inhaled the scent of the ocean and listened to the seabirds screeching as they wheeled and dipped in the gusts of wind.

Her pulse rate slowed and the knot in her stomach slowly dissolved. The sea-damp fall air was just what she had needed to cool off. Worked every time. Well, against her temper. The lust still humming in her veins was something else entirely. Usually, no matter what problem was bothering her, Jade could step out here, let the wind caress her, and she'd feel her troubles slide away. In fact, this wide, private balcony with a view of the bay was the reason she'd rented the apartment in the first place. Wouldn't you know that J.T. would be the one problem not so easily gotten rid of?

She leaned her forearms on the railing and stared down at the world below. From her home on the top floor of the three-story building, she felt as though she could see forever. The horizon stretched out before her, filled with possibilities. And from three stories up, she felt safe from...

"Don't go there," she told herself firmly. But it was too late. Her mind had already drifted into dangerous territory. It wasn't enough that work itself was becoming a problem. That J.T. had popped back into her life. No, she also had to worry about whoever it was sending her letters that were just creepy enough to make her install a new dead bolt on her apartment door.

The latest one had been delivered to her desk at work only yesterday, and she'd already memorized the contents.

My lovely Jade. Soon we will be together.
Soon the world will know, as I do, that we were
meant to be. Soon, my love, soon.

The police assured her she wasn't in serious danger. Most of these cases, they insisted, turned out to
be nothing more than an enraptured fan who didn't
have the courage to confront the object of his affection face-to-face. Still, that didn't make her feel any
better about having an unknown admirer stalking
her.

Wrapping her arms around her middle and leaning
against the weathered stone balustrade, she forced
her thoughts away from what she couldn't control
and back to the problem at hand.

Getting into the palace.

Which would entail getting past her ex-husband.
No small feat.

Just thinking about J.T. was enough to heat up
her bloodstream again, and it wasn't all due to anger. Life would have been so much easier if it were.

With the king in a coma, the public wanted to
know that their country, their interests, were being
taken care of. And it was Jade's job to investigate
that. At least, it was if she ever wanted to move
away from fluff pieces to real news. If she ever
wanted to prove to her father that— No, this wasn't
about her father. Or the baggage she carried around

with her. This was about her goals. Her plans. Her ambitions.

Something J.T. had never understood.

Now, once again, standing between her and accomplishing her task was that mountain of a man. "Nothing's changed there, has it?" she asked herself. Three years ago, he hadn't wanted her to work, either. He'd wanted a traditional wife. A woman who would have dinner on the table every night at six and be content with taking care of him and their future children.

On the surface, there was nothing at all wrong with that. But Jade wanted more. Always had. And when she couldn't get it through J.T.'s thick, chauvinistic skull that her ambitions were no less important than his, she'd stomped out of his life in a fit of righteous anger.

The only problem was, she'd left her heart behind.

Looking back now, she could see that she should have stayed and worked it out. Or at least tried. But she'd been so much younger then. So full of fire and impatience. And J.T., she conceded in her own defense, hadn't been much better.

Jade sighed heavily and faced reality. The plain fact was she'd left, determined to have a career. But now that she had it, the career she'd wanted so desperately wasn't making her happy. Maybe things would change if she actually managed to get the interview with the queen. But right now, Jade felt as though she'd made a stupid bargain when she'd given up her marriage for ambition.

Seeing him again hurt. The near electric shock of meeting his gaze was still buzzing through her brain. Almost as if she'd found something she hadn't known was lost.

"Oh, you're in sad shape," she muttered, turning away from the ocean view to go back inside. She left the glass door open, and the sheer white drapes billowed in the wind like a sail. Like her, they were anchored and going nowhere.

A knock sounded on the apartment door and she jumped. Unease skittered along her spine, but she went to answer it anyway. Any interruption at all was better than letting her brain focus on J.T. and what they'd both lost. But she froze with her hand on the knob. The days of just throwing her door open without thinking about it were over.

She peered through the peephole and sighed as she recognized her building's doorman.

"Charles?"

He stepped back and smiled, knowing that she was looking at him, then held up a manila envelope. "A package was delivered for you. From the television station. I'll just leave it outside your door."

"Thank you." Quickly, she disengaged the locks and opened the door.

Charles was already walking to the elevator.

Jade snatched up the envelope, stepped back inside and closed and locked the door again. She looked down at the envelope. From the feel of it, there was a video tape inside, and when she tore it open, she was proved right.

A piece of notepaper fell from the envelope and she bent over to pick it up. "Found this on your desk. Thought it might be important." It was signed by Janine, her secretary.

"On my desk?" Jade muttered as she walked back into the living room. There were no labels on the tape. Nothing to indicate what it might contain. But someone in the newsroom must have left it for her. Heading directly for the TV, she slipped the tape into the VCR, then turned on the set and hit Play.

An image of the palace appeared on the oversize television screen, and a chill crawled up her spine to lift the tiny hairs at the back of her neck. Traffic sounds, the call of birds and the sighing of the wind across the microphone were the only sounds. The unseen cameraman worked the zoom lens, and Jade was suddenly watching herself—with Harry, the station cameraman, right behind her—standing just outside the palace gates. She saw her own image argue with the guard, then grab the iron gate and shake it. She watched as she sent Harry back to the van, as she confronted J.T.

She relived the whole confrontation because she was simply too stunned to hit the stop button. In the video, she saw her hair ruffled by the wind. She felt the cameraman's obsession as he slowly tightened the zoom to pan in on her alone—in effect, cutting her off from J.T. and the rest of the world. Keeping her separate.

For him only.

Slowly, the camera panned from the top of her head to the sole of her tapping foot and back up again. Jade felt her stalker's obsession as if it were a living thing in the room with her. The shot tightened further, lingering on her eyes, her mouth. She could hear the cameraman's labored breathing as he watched her, and the sound nearly choked off her own air.

At last, when she was turned away from the palace gates, the tape ended, fading into a solid blue screen that finally woke her out of her stupor. She jabbed the stop button with one fingertip, then dropped the remote to the floor as if it were poisonous.

Silence crashed down around her. The drapes, still billowing in the wind, suddenly made her aware of an unsecured entry point, and Jade hurried across the room. Of course, to break into a third-story apartment through the balcony doors, her stalker would have to be Spider-Man. But it made her feel better to slam the glass door shut. She locked it, then bent down to drop the metal guard into the track behind it.

Alone and scared, she turned her back on the view and stared at her apartment. For the first time, she didn't see the comfortable, yet stylish furnishings. What she saw now was her sanctuary...*invaded* by a threat she couldn't identify.

And she wanted to call J.T. so badly, her heart ached.

There was too much going on for J.T.'s liking.

He sat in the single chair opposite his boss's desk and let his mind wander while Franklin Vancour was on the phone. In his fifties, Franklin was as fit as a man half his age. It came from years of military training, no doubt, and J.T. could appreciate that. The other man was as dedicated to duty as he was, and on that common ground, the two men understood each other.

Morning sunlight filtered in through the windows of the security office located on the ground floor of the palace. The wood-paneled walls gleamed richly from years of careful polishing. Framed certificates and royal proclamations hung on the walls, and their glass fronts winked when a stray sunbeam glanced off of them. A row of bookcases lined one wall, and hundreds of leather-bound, well-read volumes rested alongside mementos left behind by former heads of security.

The RII—Royal Intelligence Institute—was responsible for the safety and security of the royal family. The guards posted outside, as well as J.T. himself, had been plucked from the different branches of the Penwyck military and assigned to the palace. Every man here was the best of the best.

Next door was the king's office, and J.T. knew without having to be told that Sir Selwyn, the king's secretary, would be there, positioned to keep out all intruders. A thin, wiry man, he was dedicated to his employer. Even to the point of putting up with Broderick, the man who so wanted to be king of Penwyck, but never could.

But until Morgan, the rightful king, either recovered from his illness or was succeeded by one of his sons, Morgan's twin, Broderick, would remain temporarily in charge, reigning in his brother's stead.

J.T. could not understand how twin brothers could be as different from each other as the king and Broderick were. Morgan was fair-minded and loyal, with an innate sense of decency. Broderick, on the other hand, couldn't be trusted as far he could be thrown. But since it was J.T.'s sworn duty to protect the royals, he was bound to keep his opinions to himself and simply do his job.

As Franklin hung up the phone and leaned back in his black leather chair, J.T. turned to find the man studying him. "What's this I hear about you and a female reporter having a public argument at the gate yesterday?"

He shouldn't have been surprised. Not much got past Vancour. Which was why he was in charge of security around here.

"Not really an argument," J.T. countered, crossing his right foot atop his left knee. "She wanted in. I disagreed. I won."

Franklin's bushy gray eyebrows lifted slightly. "So I heard. But the point is, we can't afford to offend the press right now."

"Offend her?" J.T. almost chuckled, but he knew it wouldn't be appreciated. "With her attitude, she's lucky she didn't get shot. Lieutenant Gimble deserves a medal for putting up with her tirade."

Franklin sighed and shook his head. "Ms. Erickson is a popular personality these days."

J.T. shifted uncomfortably in his chair. He had the distinct feeling he wasn't going to like the direction this conversation was taking.

His boss continued. "The queen watches her *People in Penwyck* reports every day."

"Yeah," J.T. said. "Real in-depth reporting

there. What was her last bit? About the cats who've lived in the palace?''

"Doesn't matter," the other man countered. "The point is, your former wife's making a name for herself."

"I know." There were only a handful of people on this whole island who knew that he and Jade had once been married. They'd divorced long before she'd become an on-air personality. Vancour knew only because of the security check J.T. had had to pass before accepting the promotion to the palace guard.

But this was the first time in two years the other man had mentioned it.

"No way," J.T. muttered, suspicion crawling through him. He pushed himself out of the chair. "You're not suggesting we let her into the palace to do her interview, are you?"

"No." Franklin propped his fingertips together as he thought about it. "Not yet, anyway. Soon, though. Won't be able to avoid it much longer. What I'm suggesting is that you show her around the palace grounds for now." He shrugged. "Give her a little and maybe she'll be satisfied."

J.T. doubted that. "Not her. She wants an interview and she won't be satisfied until she gets it."

"No interviews. Yet."

There was something in his tone, an underlying edge of excitement, that caught J.T.'s attention.

"Is there news on the king?"

Franklin studied J.T. for a long minute, decided he had no qualms about telling him what he knew. Jeremy Wainwright was the most trustworthy man he'd ever known. The lad was headed for big things one day, Franklin mused. Maybe even this job.

And in this office, with the door closed, the two men could talk freely, without worrying about being overheard or quoted.

Nodding, he said, "The king's doctors seem to think there are encouraging signs. It seems he may be rousing from the coma."

"That is good news." Hell, it was great news. As a citizen of Penwyck, J.T. had been as worried about his king as anyone else. And being a member of the inner circle, he'd been a part of the coverup that had been so dangerous to his country. "So does this mean that Br—"

"No." Franklin stood up, too. "The king's brother will remain as temporary head of the country." Pacing, he seemed to be carefully considering something as he said, "And frankly, the easier we can make this on the queen, the better. Her Majesty is inundated with problems and trying to keep things running despite Broderick's interference."

J.T. nodded and waited for the man to continue. It didn't take long.

"The RET is doing what it can. But security here is up to us."

The Royal Elite Team was probably champing at the bit to do something—anything. But when it came to palace security, the RII was in charge. And J.T. was just competitive enough to enjoy knowing that the members of the RET were clearly unhappy with the situation.

"I understand," he said, though he wasn't entirely sure he knew where Franklin was going with this.

The older man laughed shortly and stopped his frenetic pacing to stare at him from across the room. "I don't think you do, or you wouldn't be so agreeable."

"What's going on, Franklin?"

"I need you to distract your ex-wife."

"That's going above and beyond the call of duty." Dumbfounded, J.T. swallowed back a rising tide of anger.

"You know her best. Know how to keep her off track. Keep her happy."

If he'd known how to keep her *happy*, J.T. thought, they'd still be married. This was a bad idea. Real bad. And he didn't mind saying so. "Won't work. Jade's not exactly my biggest fan."

"Just buy us a couple of days."

"And then what?"

"She'll get her interview and you won't have to deal with her again."

Now that should be good news. But the fact was, J.T. had done nothing but think about her since seeing her outside the gates. She'd haunted his every thought, stalked his dreams and filled his mind until he couldn't even draw a breath without imagining her scent.

Now that he'd seen her again after three long years, he wasn't exactly in a hurry to be rid of her. And that surprised him as much as it would have her.

Vancour walked across the room slowly, keeping his gaze locked with J.T.'s. "I need your cooperation in this, Wainwright. Your king needs it."

J.T. studied him. There was something in the other man's eyes that hinted at the seriousness of the situation. Well, hell, they'd all been living in a pressure cooker for weeks. Ever since the king had collapsed unexpectedly.

Placate Jade.

From a purely male standpoint, that wasn't such a tough assignment. There was so much history between them, though. So much hurt and pain and misery. Yet before the pain, there had also been…a *connection* between them that had been stronger and deeper than anything he'd ever experienced before or since.

But she also had an argumentative streak that would give the most patient man in the world the urge to throttle her. Just remembering how she'd stood up to him, shaken the iron gates and glared at him without an instant's hesitation was almost enough to make J.T. smile. A man his size didn't usually meet people who weren't instantly intimidated. Jade never had been, though, and he'd always admired her for it.

She wouldn't be an easy woman to manipulate. And if Franklin Vancour thought she could be bought off by a walk through the palace gardens, he was sadly mistaken.

Still…if all the palace required was a few more days' respite, maybe J.T. could pull it off. Maybe he could keep her busy enough that she wouldn't notice that she wasn't any closer to the interior of the palace than she'd been yesterday. And, if he spent enough time in her company, perhaps the attraction he felt for her would die a natural death. Maybe this was what they both needed to completely end what they'd finished three years ago. Maybe they needed to spend time together again to realize that it was all really gone.

And maybe he was a masochist.

At any rate, it'd certainly be the most interesting assignment he'd been given since joining the RII.

He looked at Franklin. "A few days?"

The man nodded slowly. "At the most."

"I'll do my best," J.T. told him.

"I knew I could count on you."

A few minutes later, Jeremy was letting himself out of the security office and heading back to the guardhouse. Autumn sunshine spilled out of a cloudy sky and he told himself that he should enjoy it while it lasted. He had a feeling he was headed into stormy weather.

Three

————

The next morning, J.T. sat through the security briefing, but his mind was several miles away. Five, to be exact. He imagined Jade in a plush office, snapping orders at a battalion of minions. Once she'd finished making heads roll, she would no doubt sit back in a comfortable chair, sip a morning cup of tea and plan how next she would try to ruin his life.

And she'd do it all with a smile curving that fabulous mouth of hers.

Around him, the other members of the RII shifted and muttered to one another, but as far as J.T. was concerned, they had the easy jobs. All they had to do was concern themselves with defense of the palace. Routine tasks, with only the occasional chance to jump in front of some crazed assassin. *He,* on the other hand, would soon be dealing with the only woman who'd ever been able to get to him.

His fingers tightened around the pen in his right hand. Just to torture himself, J.T. had started his day by watching her early morning report on PEN-TV. Real investigative stuff, he mused now, making a point of relaxing his hand. Jade Erickson had looked directly into the camera and, with a beaming smile on her face, reported a story on the old smugglers caves. Then she'd even launched into the local belief that ghosts of long-dead pirates still haunted the dank caverns.

His amusement had died quickly enough, though, when he reminded himself that she'd walked out on him and what they might have had together for the opportunity to smile into a camera.

Of course, he didn't want to think about just how good she'd looked, standing in the wind, with the roaring sea just behind her. How her auburn hair had flown about her face with abandon and how her sea-green eyes had seemed to stare directly into his.

All right, he thought, pushing her image out of his brain. He didn't need to think about her now. He'd be seeing her all too soon as it was.

* * *

After a sleepless night, Jade was in no mood to be stonewalled at the palace gates today. She'd thought about it long and hard during the hours she'd spent sitting straight up in bed, gripping her self-defense weapon—a golf club. For weeks now, she'd been receiving those vaguely threatening letters. Only recently had they begun to get a bit creepier. But the video stalking was definitely upping the ante.

Yet she couldn't allow this individual, whoever it was, to affect her work. If she crawled off into a hole and hid away, then the person trying to scare her would have won. Besides, there was no guarantee that hiding would protect her. Maybe it was safer to stay in the public eye. Certainly, it would be difficult, if not impossible, for someone to kidnap her out of the station. Or from in front of a news camera.

No, the thing to do was to go on with her everyday life as if nothing were wrong. To surrender was to lose power in this, and she wouldn't allow that to happen. She'd fought for a long time to have the kind of career she'd always dreamed of. She'd given up the man she loved. She'd made this choice and now she would find a way to make it work.

In fact, she hadn't even bothered to go into the station first this morning. Hadn't had to. They'd run one of her taped pieces on the morning news. She'd simply called in and had Harry meet her at her apartment. Might as well beard J.T. in his den as early as possible.

"You okay?" Harry asked as he steered the station van down the tree-lined street toward the palace.

"Dandy," she said, and tugged the hem of her camel-brown skirt over her knees.

"Well, you don't look okay."

"Gee thanks, Harry." Jade smiled at her cameraman. They'd been together for two years and Harry was her best friend at the station. "You're such a sweet-talker."

The older man grumbled unintelligibly for a minute or two, then sucked in a deep breath and blew it out again. "I only meant that you look tired."

So much for the miraculous properties of makeup. She flipped the visor down and peered at her own reflection in the small mirror. He was right. Jade sighed, flipped the visor back up and admitted, "I didn't get much sleep last night."

"Another letter?" he asked, his voice tight with worry.

"No," she said quickly, "no more letters." She'd already decided not to tell him about the videotape. The police and her bosses at the station weren't concerned about the letters she'd been receiving. But Harry, bless him, was. No point in telling him about the tape. Anyway, she had the video with her and planned to take it to the police station herself this afternoon.

Besides, it hadn't been worry keeping her up half the night. It had been dreams of J.T. Memories. His face floating through her mind and the recollection of his touch on her body… Nope. No sleep for Jade.

"That's good." Harry steered the van around a stalled car, pushed his way into the stream of traffic again, then asked, "So why are we hitting the palace bright and early? This could have waited until later."

"Maybe," she conceded, and stifled a yawn. "But why wait? If I catch him early enough in the morning, maybe he'll be off guard."

"Him?" Harry snorted a laugh and came to a stop as a gaggle of schoolchildren raced across the street, their laughter bubbling in their wake. Sliding a glance at her, the older man said, "I don't think that man's ever had his guard down."

"You don't know the half of it," she muttered, keeping her gaze fixed on the passing traffic. Anything to make her mind too busy to dredge up yet another image of J.T. "There's a first time for everything."

"Yeah," he muttered, stepping on the gas again, "and that goes for getting hit by lightning, run down by a car.…"

"That's the spirit," she said with a laugh.

Harry shook his head as he parked the van. Throwing the gearshift into Park, he cut the engine and slanted her another look. "Spirit's not going to cut it in this one, Jade. If they don't want you in the palace, you're not going to be able to charm your way in."

She stared through the windshield at the palace gates fifty feet away. Uniformed guards were positioned just outside, and through the iron scrollwork, she saw more guards marching across the compound. None of them looked friendly. But then, they weren't supposed to, were they?

This was her country, though. As a citizen of Penwyck, she had every right to enter that compound. Heck, she could sign up for a tour and get farther inside than she had yesterday. As that thought occurred to her, Jade's brain raced with possibilities. It was as though she were in a cartoon and a lightbulb had just clicked on over her head. She could pay for a tour, and then somewhere along the route through the public rooms, she could simply...get lost. If she wandered away from her tour group and just happened to stumble into the royal family's private quarters, no one could really blame her, right? After all, they didn't behead people anymore. What did she have to lose?

"Oh," Harry said softly, "I don't think I like that look in your eyes."

"I'm going to get inside the palace today," she assured the man beside her. "By hook or by crook."

"And when they arrest us?" Harry asked, his normal gloomy tone even more morose than usual.

Jade turned to look at him. Reaching out, she patted his arm and said, "We'll ask for adjoining cells."

"Now that's real comforting, thanks."

"Relax, Harry," Jade said, a slow smile curving her mouth. "When have I ever gotten us in over our heads before?"

"Let's see..." Harry held up his right hand, ticking off items on his fingers one by one. "There was the time you wanted to do an exposé on the Royal Navy and we got stuck belowdecks of that carrier when she shipped out."

She waved one hand dismissively. "They found us within hours."

"Then there was the time you wanted to do an aerial report from a hot-air balloon and you accidentally pulled the string releasing the hot air and we—"

"Made it safely down to earth," she pointed out quickly. Besides, it had been a great report. She'd had to do outrageous stunts over the last couple of years. Anything to get herself noticed, to stand out from the crowd of pretty faces looking for a shot at success.

He sent her a look from beneath raised eyebrows. "Then there was—"

"Okay," she said, holding her hands up in mock surrender. There was definitely a downside to having the same cameraman over the years. Especially one with a memory like Harry's. "You made your point. So, there've been a few unfortunate incidents."

"Unfortunate?"

"We survived."

"They say God protects fools and drunks."

She smiled wryly. "Since I don't drink, I know which category you're filing me under."

"Me, too, Jade," he said. "Though after a shoot with you, I rarely say no to a good, stiff drink."

"We got the stories though, didn't we?"

"True."

"And now we've got a shot at the big time."

His fingers tightened around the steering wheel. "Why are you making such a big deal of this, Jade? Why push for the interview now? Once the king's better, the queen'll be more than happy to talk to anyone from the press."

"That's why, Harry." Jade shifted in her seat and leaned toward him. "I have to snag this interview. It's what I've been working toward, waiting for for three years." *This is the chance I gave up my mar-*

riage for, she thought, but managed to keep that to herself. "This is my shot at proving to the powers-that-be at the station that I'm more than a fluff reporter. It's my chance at a co-anchor job."

She'd served her time on the gossip circuit. She'd done the lost-dog and hero-fireman stories. She'd covered parades and fairs and the opening of supermarkets, all the while telling herself that her time would come. That eventually, she'd have the career that had always been so important to her.

If she didn't...then she'd failed.

And she'd walked away from J.T. for nothing.

That was something she couldn't live with.

She unbuckled her seat belt, opened the door and stepped out. Slamming the door behind her, she leaned in the open window.

"I'm going to stop at the gates first. So get the camera. If we can get past J.T., er, Jeremy Wainwright, we'll do it that way." She patted the door. "Otherwise, I'll be signing up for a tour this afternoon."

"A tour? Oh, I've got a bad feeling about this."

Reaching up, she straightened the lapels of her brown suede jacket, tossed her hair back from her face and gave him one last smile. "Ignore that bad feeling. I'll meet you at the gates."

"I'll be right behind you," he said, clearly unhappy about the whole thing.

Nodding, Jade walked off, her heels clicking loudly on the leaf-strewn sidewalk as she headed for the palace gates.

Harry looked after her for a long minute, then, shaking his head, moved to get his camera. There was no stopping her, he knew. The best he could do was be close by when the you-know-what hit the fan.

She looked amazing.

Even better than he remembered. And he would have been willing to bet that wasn't possible.

J.T. watched her approach, not surprised at all that she'd shown up first thing in the morning. The woman had a head like a rock. Of course, that was a personality trait he could appreciate, being fairly hardheaded himself. He'd known yesterday that Jade would be back. She'd never been a woman to give up easily—except, of course, when it came to their marriage.

What a package she made.

That body of hers was enough to tempt a saint right out of heaven. Her hair lifted off the collar of her brown suede jacket and blew softly in the wind. He'd never understood how women could stand wearing high heels, as they looked particularly uncomfortable. But as a man, he was incredibly grateful that women were willing to put up with the discomfort. His gaze swept up her legs, enjoying the view, and when that view ended at the hem of her skirt, he lifted his gaze to hers. Even from a distance, it wasn't hard to see the glitter of determination in her sea-foam-colored eyes.

Well, she wasn't the only one who had a job to do, he told himself as he started for the gate. Distracting his ex-wife might not seem like much of an assignment, but he had never been one to question orders, either. So he'd do what Vancour expected of him. After all, no one had to know that he was almost looking forward to butting heads with Jade.

J.T. waved aside the uniformed soldier standing guard and waited for her himself. It didn't take long.

In seconds, she was standing directly opposite him. Her gaze moved over the elaborate iron gate and paused on the lock before lifting to meet his.

"Morning, J.T."

He nodded. "Jade."

She waved one hand at the gate. "I see we're still at a stalemate."

"On the contrary," he said, and had the pleasure of seeing a spark of curiosity light her eyes.

"Really?" she countered. "Because from where I stand, I still seem to be on the wrong side of the gate."

"Opposite sides, huh? The story of our lives."

"J.T...."

"Today, at least, that's easily correctable," he said, enjoying the suspicion now written across her features. In a few quick moves, he had the gate unlocked and was pushing it open just wide enough for her to slip inside.

But she didn't.

Eyes wary, she looked from the opening to him and back again before asking, "What's going on?"

He drew his head back, a look of pure innocence on his face. "Why, Jade. Don't you trust me?"

"Said the spider to the fly."

J.T. laughed. God, he'd missed her. He'd missed it all. The fights, the loving, the laughter. It had been hard as hell to get to the point where he didn't miss her every damn minute. Now here he was—about to put himself through the misery all over again.

And he couldn't wait.

He slapped one hand to his chest. "Jade, honey, you wound me."

One of her auburn eyebrows lifted in a high arch. "Not without a flamethrower, I'm thinking."

He laughed again and paid no attention to the soldier standing nearby. Stepping through the gate to the sidewalk, J.T. stopped directly in front of her. In fact, he was so close to her he swore he could feel her heat shimmering around him. He could damn sure smell her perfume. The faint flowery scent surrounded him, slipping inside him to his weakest point and attacking.

She'd probably planned that.

Shrugging it off, he lifted his gaze past her to the older man hurrying up the sidewalk, video camera clutched in his arms like a child.

She followed his gaze. "That's Harry. My cameraman. You remember him from yesterday."

"Yeah, I do." But truth to tell, Jeremy hadn't really counted on having the cameraman following them around all day. So he'd just have to get rid of the guy. Shifting his gaze to hers, J.T. said, "Look, Jade. I've been instructed that I can allow you into the palace grounds. Give you a tour of the private gardens. Show you around a little. But no camera."

She looked up at him, and he enjoyed the fact that she had to tilt her head far back to do it. His size had always been handy when trying to intimidate. Although it had never bothered her any.

"Excuse me? A tour of the gardens?" she repeated. "What about my interview with Her Majesty? J.T., I did a story on the palace gardens just last month. The people really don't care all that much if the roses are still blooming."

"It's all you get."

"I nee—*want* a hard news piece, J.T. And if I don't get it, the station'll just send another reporter."

"Is that a threat?"

"It's a promise." She gritted her teeth as she added, "Probably Vince Battle."

"Barracuda Battle?" Oh, wouldn't the palace love that? The hard-edged reporter made every interview an exposé. He dug and dug until he uncovered every last bit of dirt there was to find, and what he couldn't find he invented.

"That's the one."

"Perfect."

"Well, we agree on something, anyway. We'd both rather have *me* do this."

"Unfortunately, it's not up to either one of us."

With her right hand, she flipped the edge of her jacket back and planted her fist on her hip. She was trying like hell to hold on to her temper, and J.T. sort of admired her for the attempt. Still, he saw the sparks in her eyes and knew his Jade was alive and well. His gaze dropped briefly to the curve of that hip, then lifted slowly to appreciate the way her peach silk blouse caressed her breasts. Damn.

Scraping one hand across his face as if to wake himself up from a lust-induced coma, J.T. looked into her eyes and said, "All right. I can't promise anything, but I think if you'll be patient for a couple days…"

"Patient." She said it as if it were a word foreign to her nature.

As he knew it was. "Give it a shot, Jade. It's my best offer."

She didn't want to be patient. He could see it in her eyes, which were snapping with electricity like a storm at sea. "J.T.," she said finally, "is this the real deal or did they just tell you to give me the runaround?"

Harry stepped up behind her, but she didn't turn to look at him. She couldn't take her eyes off J.T., once her husband, now the king's pit bull. She wanted to trust him.

"Tours of the palace grounds can be…interesting," he said, and his voice held a promise of more than just a tour.

But maybe, she told herself as she fought down an urge to fan herself, she was just reading more into his body language and that voice of his than was actually there. Was it all her? she wondered. Was she the only one experiencing flashbacks of better days, happier days? Did he ever remember their too brief but amazing time together?

"So," he was asking, "do we have a deal?"

"Deal?" Harry demanded. "What kind of deal?"

Jade didn't glance at him. "No camera?"

"No cameras?" Harry sounded outraged. "This is TV, not radio!"

"That stinks." Jade looked at J.T., silently daring him to make it stick.

"That's the deal," he said. "The private areas of the palace stay private. So what do you say?"

Jade didn't glance at Harry. She knew what he'd say. The man treated his camera like an appendage. He'd expect to go inside with her. And rightly so. They were a team. On the other hand, wouldn't it be wise for her to take whatever she could get, here?

She kept her gaze locked on J.T.'s brown eyes as they stared directly into hers. She felt a...*connection* humming between them, and she wasn't at all sure what to do about it. For so long she'd wondered what it would be like to meet up again with the man she'd loved so desperately. And now that it had finally happened, there was a cowardly part of her that wanted to run and hide. But she'd run three years ago, and that hadn't brought her any peace. So this time she'd stand her ground and never let him know that he could still turn her knees to jelly. Now if only she could keep her hormones from zinging to life whenever she was around the man.

But that, she thought with an inward sigh, was a faint hope.

Okay, she'd take his tour. She didn't have much choice, did she? It was take this deal or go pay her five pounds at the palace tour entrance. And at least with J.T. guiding her through the place, she'd see more than the public rooms and gardens. Plus, she considered, still meeting his gaze squarely, she could always slip away from him as easily as she could from a tour guide.

With that thought firmly in mind, she said, "Harry, go on back to the station. I'll grab a cab when I'm finished here."

Harry grumbled, but ambled off.

A moment later, Jade held out her right hand and said sweetly, "It's a deal, J.T."

Then his hand took hers and a burst of heat skittered along the length of her arm to shatter in her chest, splintering her veins with a liquid warmth that surprised her.

And by the look in his eyes—her touch had the same effect on him.

Four

J.T. felt the loss the instant Jade snatched her hand back. The heat on his fingers lingered, a warmth he hadn't known in three long years. Looking into her eyes, he saw that she'd felt it, too, but was just as determined as he to ignore it. Fine by him. She'd shot him out of the sky once—he wasn't about to let it happen again.

Strange that they'd come together again after all this time. And wouldn't you know that it would happen *because* of the choice she'd made years ago? She'd given him up for dreams of a career. Now that career had brought her into direct opposition with his.

"Jade?" the cameraman called to her, and when she turned to talk to the older man, J.T. kept his eyes on both of them.

"Look, Harry," she was saying, with a brief glimpse over her shoulder at J.T., "I'm going in to do the tour. See what I can find out."

"Without film to show, what good's the tour going to do us?"

Jade hooked her arm through Harry's and pulled him a bit farther away, to make sure they wouldn't be overheard. "I'll get something. Right now, I'm going to play the game. Don't worry about it. We'll get film before we're finished."

Harry glanced over her shoulder at the big man standing at the open palace gate, then shifted his gaze back to hers. "I don't think this one's going to be easy to get around, Jade."

J.T. never had been, she thought. Checking her watch, she said, "I'll see you back at the station in a couple of hours, okay?"

Harry agreed reluctantly, then turned and headed off toward the van. She watched him go and briefly wished she were going with him. Suddenly, the idea of sitting at the station planning next week's show sounded a lot better to her than spending the next couple of hours with J.T. Still, he was her way into the palace, and she needed that interview. Nodding to herself, Jade walked back to the gates and stopped directly in front of the man. "Are you ready?" she asked.

"As I'll ever be," he muttered, then took a step back and waved her through the gates.

An hour and a half later, Jade had seen enough rosebushes and statuary to last her a lifetime. Oh, the private gardens were beautiful. Every last blade of grass was trimmed neatly. No stray leaves were left to scatter color on the stone pathways. Each rose bloomed to perfection and even the sunlight seemed more polished in this sheltered enclosure. Marble statues, carved centuries before, stood as beautiful and pristine as the day the sculptor had completed his work. Water splashed in the fountains and a soft sea breeze slipped over the high stone walls surrounding the palace.

And she didn't care about any of it.

Her gaze slid to the glass walls fronting on the garden. Behind that painfully clean glass lay the private quarters of the royal family. The people she needed to reach.

So near and yet so far.

J.T. never left her side. Like the old days, a quiet voice in her mind insisted. She remembered so clearly the evening walks they used to take along the coast road. Knowing he was there, right beside her, had filled her with a sense of peace and safety and hunger that she hadn't known since. Now, though, it was different, just as they were different. There was no intimacy between them. Just hazy memories of a brief marriage that probably never should have happened in the first place.

"The marble used in the statues was quarried in the Aronleigh Mountains," he was saying, and Jade stopped in her tracks to look up at him. "What?" he asked.

"I already know about the sculptures."

"Sorry."

He didn't look sorry. He looked amused. As if he was enjoying her frustration at getting the runaround. So much for fond memories and songs of yesteryear.

"J.T...." She waved both arms toward the gardens and said, "This is all lovely. But every child in Penwyck learns about the palace in school."

"Ah, but not every schoolchild gets a tour of the private gardens, now do they?"

"A rose is a rose is a rose," Jade said.

Nodding, he shoved both hands into his pants pockets and inhaled deeply enough to swell his broad chest to immense proportions. "Yeah, I know. I'm bored, too."

"Then why are we doing this?"

"Because you won't go away," he said flatly,

giving her a look that told her he wished to hell she would.

There was a time when that would have been the last thing on his mind. Jade walked over to a nearby stone bench and took a seat beside the closest fountain, a marble dolphin spraying water from its mouth. Barely glancing at it, she lifted her gaze to J.T.'s and said, "I *can't* go."

"You didn't have this much trouble leaving three years ago."

"How long are you going to throw that in my face?"

"How much time do we have?"

"For God's sake, J.T." She crossed her legs, smoothed the hem of her skirt down over her knees and clasped her fingers there tightly, as if to keep herself from flinging her hem up over her head and begging him to take her. Now. *Oh, good God, where did that come from?* Pushing the thought out of her brain, she tightened the leash on her temper. Surely that was a better bet than slavering all over him. "We were kids."

"You were twenty-five," he countered. "I was twenty-nine. Too old to be kids."

"You were born old," she said.

"That's nice."

"You know what I mean." Jade waved his pretend hurt feelings aside. "You always knew where you were going. What you wanted. I'd just gotten out of college. I didn't know anything.''

It had taken her years longer to get her degree than most people. She'd taken classes in fits and starts, working to put herself through school. Then, just after graduation, she'd met J.T. and been swept up into a whirlwind of lust and love and promises of a future. Three months later, they were married. Four weeks after that, Jade had walked out, and nothing had ever been the same since.

''You knew you wanted to marry me,'' he muttered, and took a seat beside her.

She shook her head and slanted him a look. ''I knew I wanted you. More than my next breath. You sashayed me into marriage before I knew what hit me.''

''Ah,'' he said, leaning back and stretching incredibly long legs out in front of him. ''So this is my fault.''

''I didn't say that.''

''Sure you did. I tricked you into marrying me.''

''No, you just kissed me into it.'' Disgusted with herself, Jade shifted, leaned back against the bench and folded her arms over her chest.

He'd entranced her so completely, so thoroughly, she'd have moved to the moon if he'd said, ''Let's go.'' So what did that say about her? That she was weak? Well, maybe she was. At least where J.T. was concerned.

Or she *had* been.

She'd grown up since then.

Right?

"It wasn't anybody's fault," she finally said, her voice barely audible above the splashing water beside her. "It just didn't work out."

"Because you didn't try."

"Because I wasn't willing to do things *your* way."

"Really?" he challenged with a snort. "You consider a four-week marriage to be a real test of a relationship?"

"Come on, J.T., admit it. You wanted me to be a stay-at-home wife and mom, and you wouldn't listen when I told you I needed more."

"I wanted to take care of you."

"I can take care of myself."

"You didn't even try to compromise. Didn't give us a shot."

"J.T., you didn't know the meaning of the word *compromise*. It was your way or the highway. I chose the highway."

"I'm not the one who walked out, Jade."

Her temper soared to the surface and frothed in a wild tangle at the base of her throat. Jade clenched her teeth tightly to keep from spilling it out in a furious tirade. Damn it. How did he *do* it? How did he push her so far, so fast?

No one else had ever been able to push her buttons the way J.T. could. And it looked as if three long years hadn't lessened his abilities any. But even if he hadn't learned anything during their time apart, *she* had.

Shaking her head, she only looked at him and said, "I'm not doing this with you, J.T. Not now." She stood up, preferring to fight on her feet. And the first order of business was to steer this conversation back onto safe territory.

"I'm here to do a job, J.T. Not fight with you." She inhaled slowly, deeply, and felt the cool, damp air fill her lungs and ease away the heat inside. "This could all be very simple."

He stood up, too, no doubt hoping to cow her with his size. Good luck with that, she thought.

"If we give you what you want."

The rumble of his voice did some very weird things to the pit of her stomach, but she refused to think about that at the moment. "Would that be so terrible?"

He threw both hands high, then let them drop down against his thighs again. "Has it ever occurred to you that there might be reasons why the royals don't want to do interviews right now?"

"The public—"

"Has a right to know." He finished the statement for her and held up one hand to keep her from saying anything else. "Yeah, I know. You guys pull that line every time you're getting stonewalled."

"It's true," she said.

"Maybe," he acknowledged, then looked her directly in the eye. "But maybe people should be allowed some privacy, too."

Jade laughed shortly. "The royal family aren't 'people.' They're news."

"They're people first, lady."

Jade paced back and forth in front of him, listening to the click of her own heels on the paving stones beneath her feet. She and J.T. were rehashing an argument they'd already had. It was still safer than talking about their shared history and what a mess they'd made of everything. "It's not like I'm trying to do some tacky exposé," she said.

"Depends on your definition of 'tacky,' doesn't it?"

"What's so terrible about wanting to talk to *my* queen to find out how *my* king is? To make sure that my country is safe? To let my fellow citizens know that they don't have to worry?"

"Oh," J.T. said, moving to intercept her as she turned to backtrack. She almost smashed into his chest, but he reached up and caught her shoulders in his big hands. "So that's what this is about," he said. "Altruistic, are you? You don't care about ratings or getting your face in front of a camera. You're just doing this for your fellow citizens?"

She felt the imprint of each of his fingers, right through the fabric of her jacket, as if he was branding her with his own personal heat. Just as he'd branded her before. It took her a second or two to unscramble the wires in her brain long enough to reply.

"You're right," she said. "It's not just because I think the people should know what's going on. This is my job. And my chance to build the career I—" She broke off and let her gaze slide from his.

"—left me for?"

"J.T."

"Fine. Sorry. We won't go there right now." He didn't let her go, and for some reason, Jade was in no hurry to break the contact between them. She stood, caught securely in his grasp, and even while she talked, a part of her simply enjoyed the heat flowing from his hands into her body.

God, it had been so long. Now, with tendrils of warmth spiraling through her, she realized that it was the first time in three long years she hadn't felt cold to the bone. Her mouth went dry and her knees trembled. Everything in her screamed at her to move closer. To step into his embrace and feel his arms slide around her, pressing her to him. She wanted to lay her head on his chest and hear that steady beat of his heart. She wanted to recall what it had been like to fall asleep like that, secure in his arms.

And because she wanted it so badly, she fought the craving fiercely.

Shaking her hair back from her face, she looked up at him and said, ''Don't you think the people of Penwyck are curious about what's going on in here? Our king is in a coma and his brother is standing in for him. Prince Dylan just returned and Princess Megan is pregnant. This is *news*, J.T. The country's buzzing and no one will talk to the press.''

J.T. let her go and she staggered back a step or two before catching herself. Damn it, he couldn't do it. Couldn't touch her without wanting—needing—more. And he couldn't have it. She was lost to him. As surely as she had been the day she'd walked out of their tiny apartment with only one sad glance for a goodbye.

He reached up and shoved one hand through his hair. This was expecting too much. His boss should never have assigned him to Jade. This was going way above and beyond the call of duty.

She was right about one thing, though. Things were in a mess around here. And it was up to men like him to keep a lid on what could be Pandora's latest boxful of trouble. One more wild story coming out of the palace and there would be even more chaos.

"Let's go," he said suddenly, and reached for her. Grabbing her elbow in a tight grip, he practically dragged her in his wake.

"Go where?" she asked, even as she hurried to keep up with him.

"Somewhere we can talk without me worrying about you trying to sneak into the damn palace."

The look on her face told him he'd struck a nerve. He'd known from the moment she'd agreed to a no-camera tour that her plan would be to get away from him and wander around on her own. But J.T. had served his time in the military and had come up against foes tough enough to prepare him for time spent with a news-hungry reporter.

Even Jade.

Now he just had to figure out how much he could give her that would ease her appetite and still protect the people in his charge.

An hour later, they were still driving. The landscape whizzed past, and Jade's fingers curled around the armrest on the passenger side door. She slid a glance at the driver of the low-slung convertible sports car and felt her breath hitch in her chest. He still drove too fast. And it still made her blood pound to be beside him as he rocketed along the coast road.

Both hands on the wheel, he steered his car around the curves with a practiced ease that made her remember how good he'd been at steering her toward climaxes that shattered her soul. Her stomach skittered as the cold autumn wind rushed at them. She shouldn't be thinking like that. Shouldn't indulge herself with vivid recollections of his hands on her body.

Then he trailed his long fingers along the leather-wrapped steering wheel and she shivered, remembering the feel of his fingertips tracing her spine.

Oh, boy.

She was in big trouble.

If she had any sense at all, she'd throw the car door open and jump out. Then she glanced at the speedometer. Nearing ninety. Okay, maybe not.

Conversation was impossible over the roar of the engine, so she kept her mouth shut and her gaze fixed on the scenery whizzing past. It was far safer than looking at J.T., after all.

But then the car began to slow as he downshifted, and she shifted her gaze in time to watch J.T. pull the car off the main road and into a parking lot in front of a small, stone pub. Weatherbeaten ivy crawled up the side and front of the building, nearly obliterating the sign that read Lion Heart, and smoke poured from the chimney on the far wall. Alongside the pub stood a house where she knew the owner lived. Open land stretched out behind the pub, and before it lay the ribbon of road, and beyond that, the ocean.

When J.T. cut the engine and yanked on the brake, the silence was instant. Yet below the quiet was the murmur of the sea and the soft sigh of the wind.

She turned in her seat to face him. "Why here, J.T.?"

He reached up, pulled off his sunglasses and gave her a half smile. "Why not here, Jade? Worried?"

"No," she said, though it was a lie. She was worried. She was being sucked back into J.T.'s world and she knew that leaving it again would kill her.

He was out of the car in a second or two and around to her side before she'd had a chance to open her door. He held it for her as she swung her legs out. Her tight, straight skirt inched high on her thighs as she scooted forward, and she tugged at it before looking up into dark-brown eyes alight with appreciation.

A slow smile curved his lips. "You may be a pain, Jade, but you've still got great legs."

Oh, God.

He held out one hand to help her up, and when she took it, he curled his fingers around hers, rubbing his thumb across her knuckles until Jade's knees wobbled dangerously. With her brain dazzled, her hormones doing a happy dance, she stepped around the car door, and when he slammed it shut, she pulled her hand free of his and tried to smooth her hair down.

"This is a mistake, J.T."

He shrugged. "Wouldn't be the first I've made."

"Me, either." The wind gusted and she pulled the edges of her jacket together across her chest. With nothing to slow it down, the wind out here raced along like an invisible freight train.

Jade sighed, shot the pub a quick look, then turned her gaze back to him. "Why are we here?"

"To talk."

Uh-huh. "About what?"

"Why don't we just get started and see where we end up?"

A woman could take that statement a couple of different ways, Jade thought. Her stomach squirmed again and her mouth went dry as she stared into those brown eyes. They were deep and dark, and the glint of something just a little wicked was enough to start a flicker of warmth deep inside her.

Just like the old days.

Darn it.

Why couldn't the palace have assigned a short,

geeky, older guy to placate her? Why did it have to be him?

"So?" he challenged. "You up for it?"

She shifted her gaze from him to the pub's scarred oak door and back again. This was his home ground. And by association, it had once been hers.

Going inside would probably be a stupid move. But if she just stood here for another five minutes, she'd freeze to death. Then they could plant her in the private gardens as yet another sculpture....

Bottom line, she'd have to take her chances. She could handle herself. J.T. wasn't the first man to send her hormones nuts.

No, her brain warned, he's just the first one to make your blood boil with a look.

"What's wrong, Jade?" he asked. "Do I worry you?"

She swallowed hard and lifted her chin. "Do I look worried?"

His gaze swept her up and down. "You look..." he paused for a long minute, then said, "like trouble."

"Maybe you should keep that in mind."

One corner of his mouth twitched. "Trust me, honey," he said, "that's one thing I'm unlikely to forget."

They headed for the pub, and the instant the door swung open, Jade was enveloped in warmth and so many familiar scents and sounds it was like coming home. Across the room, a huge fire blazed on an open hearth. A few people were seated at the small, round tables scattered across the worn but polished wooden floor. Bench seats lined the smoke-darkened stone walls, and on the far side of the room, a waist-high bar opened into the kitchen beyond.

"Have a seat," J.T. said. "What would you like to drink?"

"White wine."

He nodded, walked to the bar and slapped one hand atop it. Leaning across, he shouted, "Michael! You've got customers."

None of the customers paid any attention to J.T., or to the shouted response that came from a distance. "Is that you, J.T., boy?"

Almost instantly, a short, chubby, balding man with round red cheeks and a grin that spread across his face appeared behind the counter. Reaching across it, he slapped J.T. on the shoulder.

"Good to see you, boy. You don't get out here much anymore."

"Busy," J.T. muttered, but his deep voice carried through the room with no trouble.

"Ah yes, life at the palace," the little man said, then pointed at one of his other customers. "See you, David? This is my brother's son, J.T. Works at the palace, he does. Keeping an eye on things."

"Is that right then?" the man asked. "And the king, how is he?"

J.T. frowned to himself. *The public has the right to know.* Maybe Jade was right. Maybe the people of Penwyck did deserve to know more than they were being told. But it wasn't up to him to make that decision.

"Well, he can't be talking to the likes of you and keep his job, now can he?" Michael Wainwright countered. Then, turning back to his nephew, he asked, "What can I get for you?"

"A pint for me and a glass of white wine for the lady." He nodded his head in Jade's direction, and she watched the older man's sly smile broaden.

"Jade! By thunder it's good to see you, darlin'."

"Hello, Michael," she said, and smiled at the man who had once been family. His features creased into a broader grin and she felt herself return it. How could she not?

For three years she'd tried to keep from looking back. And now she was right smack in the middle of her past. Her gaze slid to J.T., and the warmth in his eyes reached across the room, across the years, and dipped down deep inside her.

And she didn't know how she would ever survive the cold again.

Five

"**T**wo out of three," J.T. said, and the scowl on his face told her he still couldn't believe she'd beaten him at darts.

"Well, I see you still haven't perfected your gracious-loser skills." Jade gave him a sweet smile, but didn't bother to hide the gleam of victory shining in her eyes.

He stomped across the room, snatched the metal-tipped darts out of the board and walked back to her. Handing over the blue ones, he tightened his grip on the red and said, "I don't like losing."

No, he never had. J.T. was more accustomed to

bending things—or people—to his will, than sub-
mitting himself. He'd always been larger than life.
Filled with enough confidence for three healthy people, he crashed through life full speed ahead. He'd
been a highly decorated soldier before being re-
cruited for the RII. And his advancement within the
institute's ranks was legendarily quick. He expected
the best from himself and those around him, and he
generally got it. J.T. was a man who knew what he
wanted when he saw it—and then he went after it.

Just as he'd gone after her.

A flutter in her chest told Jade that her heartbeat
was doing its weird little J.T. dance again, and she
deliberately tried to bring it under control. Without
much success. There was just something about him
that sent her cells into overdrive. It was one of those
pesky little facts of life—like gravity.

She took her darts from him and her fingertips
brushed across the palm of his hand, igniting yet
another series of small fires in her bloodstream. *Ignore it,* she told herself. Shouldn't be much more
difficult than ignoring an avalanche.

Oh, boy.

She cleared her throat, took a deep breath and
asked suddenly, "Why should I give you two out
of three? I've already won."

"Could have been a fluke," he challenged.

"It wasn't."

"Prove it."

Jade's gaze narrowed on him. "You know darn well I beat you fair and square, J.T."

He inhaled slowly, deeply, filling his lungs and swelling his broad chest once more.

Jade's heart did the flutter dance again.

"My concentration was off."

She laughed. "This is pitiful. You just can't admit that I won."

"I play better when there's a prize at stake."

Suspicion flooded her. "What kind of prize?"

He leaned in, looming over her until she was forced to tilt her head back to keep from clunking their foreheads together. Keeping his voice low and intimate, he said, "We could play for the same stakes we used to."

Heat.

Good God, she was burning up.

Jade dragged in a shaky breath but still managed to glare at him. "There is no way I'm going to do that."

"Scared?" His voice came lower, rough and hushed, a scrape of sound that skittered along her spine and then slipped deep inside her.

Swallowing hard, Jade shot a look over her shoulder at the other patrons in the pub. They were far enough away that she felt comfortable whispering, "I am *not* going to play for sex."

One dark eyebrow lifted and his mouth curved in a slow, sexy smirk. "Not just sex, babe. Hot, soul-stirring, mind-bending sex—any way the winner wants it for as long as he or she wants it."

Her body went into damp heat mode.

Her mouth went dry.

And everything inside her curled up and whimpered.

"Remember?" he whispered.

She'd have to be dead to *not* remember.

One time, she'd lost a bet purposely, just so she could enjoy pleasuring him all afternoon. Her mind filled with images of sun-spattered sheets and a soft wind caressing damp, naked flesh. She could almost feel his breath, warm on her cheek. Taste his mouth. Feel his skin beneath her palms.

"You do remember then," he said, moving in closer until she felt surrounded by him.

"Yeah." Somehow, she found the strength to squeeze that one word out of a tight throat.

"Then you probably remember what happened the last time you beat me at darts."

She swayed and closed her eyes, reliving that long summer night when J.T. had fulfilled her every wish by taking her with his mouth, over and over again. Until she lay exhausted and pleading with him to stop and let her catch her breath.

And still he hadn't stopped. He'd taken her higher

and faster and—*don't,* she told herself. Don't remember. Don't let the past overtake the present. What they'd had three years ago was gone.

"Don't do this, J.T."

His right hand curled around her upper arm, and Jade was grateful for the support even though his touch skittered through her like fireworks exploding in a night sky.

"What we had was good, Jade."

She lifted her gaze to his. "For a while."

"Why'd you leave? Why'd you give up on us?"

"You know why," she said, her voice strengthening with purpose and resolve. Pulling out of his grasp, she took a step back on shaky legs.

He shoved his free hand into his pocket, and with the other fingered the steel tips of the darts clenched in a tight fist. A muscle in his jaw twitched a couple of times and Jade knew he was fighting to maintain control. After a few seconds, he seemed to manage.

"So, we gonna play again?"

"I don't want to play games with you, J.T." A simple sentence that she knew could be taken two ways. That was fine with her. She meant it both ways.

"Maybe I let you win," he said.

"Hah!" She actually laughed out loud at the idea. "Not likely."

"How will you be sure if we don't play again?"

"If I do, and I win...*again*," she said, "what's my reward?"

He chuckled and shook his head. "Not a chance that you can beat me again."

"Uh-huh. But if I do?"

"Isn't winning its own reward?"

"Not necessarily," she said.

He folded his arms across his chest and looked down at her warily. "Fine. If you won't play for the old stakes, what've you got in mind?"

"My interview."

J.T. laughed outright then, and even though it irritated her, she had to admit that she liked the deep, booming sound. God, his laugh used to shake the windows in that rattletrap apartment they'd shared.

"You're not going to let go of this, are you?"

"Thought we'd covered that already."

"So we have," he said, the smile fading from his features slowly. "As to the interview, I'm not the one who can give you the okay on it."

"But you could put in a good word for me."

"I could."

"So then," Jade said, stroking one fingertip along the length of one of the darts, "I guess it all boils down to...are you game enough to make the bet? Or are you too worried that I'll beat the pants off—ah...win again?"

J.T.'s gaze dropped to her hands, and something

inside him tightened as he watched her slowly caress that dart. Images flashed through his mind, visions of the two of them lying upon tangled sheets, so tightly wrapped up in each other that hours passed without notice. He remembered exactly what her hands felt like on his skin and how the near electrical charge of touching her always hit him as hard as it had the first time.

His memory was good. Too good. He recalled everything. Her scent, her taste, the sweet soft sighs she made just as she peaked. And how her body welcomed his, taking him deep within her warmth and cradling him in a kind of love he'd never known before or since.

He sucked in air like a drowning man and banished those images as fast as he could.

Tearing his gaze from her hands, he looked up into those incredible eyes of hers and measured his chances. She was pretty good at this, but he'd had three long, lonely years in which to practice. He'd been working on his game, subconsciously trying to beat her even though she wasn't around anymore. Well, here was his chance to prove to himself—and to her—that he could.

J.T. had never turned down a challenge in his life. But at the same time, he had to wonder what would happen if the unthinkable did happen and she actually beat him again.

"Worried?" she asked, one corner of that delectable mouth curving into a half smile filled with confidence.

"No way." He dismissed the doubts racing through his mind.

"Then it's a bet."

He glanced from her to the dartboard and back again. "Oh yeah. It's a bet."

"Excellent," she said, grinning now like a child given the keys to a candy factory. "After our game, we can arrange a time for the interview."

"Don't sound so cocky, babe," he warned, and reached out to chuck her chin with his fingertips. "A lucky win doesn't make you a champion."

"Luck?" She shook her head and stepped back. "Luck doesn't have a thing to do with it."

"Uh-huh," J.T. said. "But about our bet. What do I get when *I* win?"

One russet eyebrow lifted slightly as she gave him a slow look. "I picked my prize...why don't you pick yours?"

Instantly, his gaze swept over her as all kinds of possibilities flashed through his mind. She seemed to have no trouble reading exactly where his thoughts were headed, since she cleared her throat and said, "Within reason, of course."

Nothing he wanted from her was reasonable, but

he heard himself say, "Dinner. My place. You cook."

She laughed, and the soft, musical sound settled over him like a promise.

"That's no prize, J.T. You remember what a terrible cook I am."

"I'll risk it."

"You like taking risks, don't you?"

"You never get anywhere without a risk or two."

"And if it blows up in your face?" she asked, suddenly wondering if they were still talking about that interview or not.

"Then at least you have the satisfaction of knowing you tried."

Satisfaction. That word hung in the still air between them and Jade shivered slightly as thoughts having nothing to do with darts filled her mind. The rest of the room seemed to drift away until it was only the two of them in that darkened, shadow-filled pub.

Oh, it had been a mistake coming here with him. She'd have done better if she'd stayed outside and frozen into statuary. At least then her heart wouldn't be twisting and her body wouldn't be going up in steam.

Seeing him again was hard. Seeing him again away from the palace was harder still. She'd been to this pub many times with J.T. She'd thought of

Michael as her own uncle. She'd worked the bar and helped serve drinks. She'd sat by the fire and dreamed silly dreams. Here, away from the palace, J.T. seemed more approachable—and that wasn't necessarily a good thing. But it was too late now to change anything. Their course was set.

So to avoid being dragged more fully into a reenactment of their past, she *had* to win their little tournament. It wasn't just to get the interview now. It was to keep J. T. Wainwright at as safe a distance as possible.

"Who goes first then?" she asked suddenly, tearing her concentration away from the thoughts careening wildly through her brain.

"Ladies, naturally," he said, and half bowed.

Nodding, she aimed and tossed her first dart. It hit the board with a solid thunk, just outside the bull's-eye.

Two hours later, he parked his car in front of the television station and switched off the engine. Turning in his seat, he glared at her. "Three out of five."

Jade laughed and shook her head. "No way. A deal's a deal, J.T."

"I still can't believe you beat me," he muttered with a shake of his head. "Nobody's beaten me in years."

"I was motivated." Whether she was more motivated to get the interview or to stay out of his apartment, she wasn't sure. But it didn't really matter, did it?

"So was I," he said, his voice a deep rumble of sound that snaked along her spine to settle low in the pit of her stomach.

Okay, she told herself, *outta the car.*

She opened the passenger door, stepped out and whipped her head to one side, snapping her windblown hair out of her eyes. "What about our deal, J.T.? Are you going to stick to it?"

His fingers tightened around the steering wheel. "I said I'd see what I could do."

"Then I'll see you tomorrow."

"Tomorrow?" He shot her a look through narrowed eyes. "I didn't say anything about tomorrow."

"Whether you come through or not, I'll be at the palace tomorrow. And every day after," she promised, leaning forward, "until I get that interview."

"And you called *me* a pit bull."

Jade laughed and eased back from the car. He looked totally disgruntled and she couldn't blame him. "See you then."

"Yeah," he muttered, then fired up the engine, threw the car into gear and swung back into the stream of traffic.

The sidewalks were crowded. People bustled past, and slowly, Jade turned to join the flow. She hadn't taken more than a step or two toward the building before she felt the hair at the back of her neck prickle.

A bone-deep chill started at the back of her shoulders and went straight down her spine. Her stomach flip-flopped. Her mouth went dry and breath staggered in and out of her lungs. *He* was there. Her stalker. He was there. In the crowd.

Somewhere.

Close by.

And he was watching her.

Spinning around quickly, Jade held her breath and scanned the faces of the people pushing past her. But there were just too many of them. And she didn't know who she was looking for. It could be anyone, from the old man on the bus bench to the young guy with long hair leaning against a phone booth.

Tears burned the backs of her eyes. Whether they were from fear or anger or both, she wasn't sure. Her stomach pitched and rolled and even her knees went wobbly. Who was it? she wondered. Which one of these people was responsible for the letters? The tape?

Suddenly feeling much too vulnerable, Jade

turned her back on all of them and hurried across the sidewalk, escaping into the safety of the Penwyck TV building.

"She's not going to give up, Franklin," J.T. said, pacing the floor in his boss's office. He'd come right back to the palace after dropping Jade at the station. But distancing himself physically from her hadn't wiped her from his mind. In fact, he could still smell her perfume, as if it was clinging to his clothes, reminding him of the hours spent in her company.

As if he needed reminding.

"I didn't expect she would," his boss said, pouring himself a cup of coffee from the insulated carafe on the corner of his desk. "Coffee?"

J.T. stopped, shook his head and said, "No, thanks."

"Suit yourself." Franklin Vancour leaned back in his maroon leather chair and studied the man opposite him.

"She wants an interview, and maybe the best thing to do here would just be to give it to her so she'll ease up."

"That's quite a turnaround," Franklin said.

"Yeah, well..." J.T. stopped in front of the desk. "She's stubborn. And smart." And a dart hustler, he told himself silently. But that didn't have anything to do with this. Sure, he'd lost a bet. But if he didn't think it was in the best interests of his country, he wouldn't be speaking up on her behalf.

Much as he hated to admit it, Jade had made some good points. The rumors flying about the king were only going to get worse if somebody didn't address them. And if she was serious about the station sending that Barracuda in if she failed, then it was in everyone's best interests to oblige Jade.

She might be a reporter, but she had scruples.

"Everyone knows the king is sick. We're only feeding the rumor mills by shutting the press out entirely."

"True." Franklin sat forward and set his coffee cup down precisely in the middle of his desk blotter. "We'd hoped to give it a few more days. But frankly, the longer we wait, the worse it looks."

"Exactly." J.T. pushed one hand through his hair. Rumors were flying and had been for weeks. Not only outside the palace, either. The guards, the soldiers, even a few members of the royal family were still in the dark as to the king's condition. "You said the queen likes Jade's reports."

"Yes, the queen enjoys her work."

"So who better to do the first interview?"

"I spoke to Her Majesty this morning, as a matter of fact," Franklin said. "And she agrees with you."

"You don't?"

"Not entirely," Franklin admitted. "I have a

healthy aversion to members of the press. Good news seldom follows a press conference or an interview session. But my opinion doesn't matter in this. The queen has decided to grant a brief interview in the hopes of easing the fears of our citizens."

"When?"

"Tomorrow morning," he said, reaching for his coffee cup again and pausing to take a deep drink. "Have your ex-wife here by nine."

J.T. looked at him long and hard for a minute. "I hope you know my opinion isn't based on the fact of my past relationship to Jade."

"I know." Vancour looked tired. He eased back in his chair again and cradled that coffee cup as if needing its heat. "But it doesn't hurt, either. At least there's one reporter we can count on to do an honest job of it."

As J.T. left the office and walked down the long hall leading to the front of the palace, he thought about his boss's words. Yeah, she was honest. Painfully so. Three years ago, she'd looked him dead in the eye and told him love wasn't enough.

Six

"**Y**ou're here early."

Startled out of her daydreams, Jade jumped and half turned in her chair. "Janine." She slapped one hand to her chest and felt the thundering beat of her own heart. "Geez, you scared me half to death."

Her assistant laughed and plopped down onto the chair opposite Jade's desk. "Sorry. Didn't mean to. You must have really been concentrating."

Hmm. Concentrating? No. Completely focusing on the mental image of being naked in J.T.'s bed? Yes.

Oh, boy.

It was a good thing Janine was efficient, capable and unable to read minds. How embarrassing was this? Behaving like some love-struck teenager. It had been a long time since Jade's hormones had been this stirred up. Actually, it had been since the last time she saw J.T. What was it about that man that could get to her so completely? So quickly?

"Hey!"

Jade blinked and realized that her assistant was waving a hand in front of her eyes. "What are you doing?"

"Just what I was going to ask you." Janine sat back in her chair and folded her arms across her chest. "You zoned out on me there."

"Sorry." Jade pushed her hair back from her face, then reached for her cup of coffee. She took a sip, shuddered and nearly gagged.

"Cold, is it?"

"Beyond cold," Jade assured her. "It's moved into the frigid and truly terrifying world."

"Want more?"

"A barrelful ought to do it." Jade looked at the woman opposite her. They'd worked together for two years now, and in that time they'd become friends. Janine was every bit as ambitious as Jade had been when she started. She saw herself in the slightly younger woman. Not just her attitude and her drive. But there was even a strong resemblance between the two of them. Janine's shoulder-length hair was almost the same color as Jade's, and they were built alike, as well. Like sisters separated at birth, Jade had often thought. And as the thought came again, she wondered if her life would have been different, easier, if she'd had a sister.

Another female in the house of testosterone.

When Jade was eight, her mother had died, and Jade's father, never very comfortable around his only daughter, had distanced himself even further. It wasn't as though he hated her or anything. It was simply that Bill Erickson didn't have a clue as to how to raise a girl. Instead, he'd focused on his four sons, and Jade had spent the rest of her life trying to be enough like her older brothers that her father would notice her, too.

Naturally, it hadn't worked.

"Hello?" Janine called, and it was clear from her tone it wasn't the first time.

"Huh?" Shaking her head, Jade said, "Wow. I really need more coffee, huh? I just seem to be wandering today."

"No problem." Janine stood up, smoothed the skirt of her navy-blue suit and asked, "How about if I sneak out and run over to the latte shop around the corner?"

"Oh God," Jade said, leaning her forearms on

her cluttered desk. "For a steaming hot mocha, you can name your price."

Janine grinned. "The chance to help edit when you get the interview with the queen?"

There was that ambition again. "You're on."

"Great." Janine turned and started for the door. After a few steps, she stopped and looked back over her shoulder. "Hey, is it okay if I borrow your coat? I left mine in my car and it's freezing out there."

"Sure, go ahead. And thanks again. But for the use of my coat, I demand at least a grande."

"No biggie," Janine assured her. "Back in a flash."

Alone again, Jade turned to her pile of notes. Picking up a pen, she made a couple of notations on the page of questions she had for the queen. There wasn't a doubt in Jade's mind that she'd get the interview. It was just a matter of time.

Her cell phone rang and before she answered it, she glanced at the incoming phone number, but didn't recognize it. Intrigued, she pushed the send button and said, "Hello?"

"Jade."

The sound of J.T.'s voice sent a conga line of goose bumps rippling along her spine. She shivered, swallowed hard and demanded, "How did you get this number? It's unlisted. Private."

"Remember where I work?"

"Oh." The palace. So what? Did that give the palace security men the right to track down private citizens at will?

Apparently.

"Well, what do you want, J.T.?" That's the way, Jade, she told herself. Attack. That'll help.

"Still charming in the morning, huh?"

She closed her eyes and took a long, deep breath. She would *not* let him get to her. She would not be drawn down memory lane one more time. Hell, she'd spent most of last night tossing and turning, her body on fire for a touch it hadn't felt in three long years. She wasn't going to do it again today.

But she also couldn't afford to tick him off. At least not until she'd gotten inside the palace. Forcing a smile, she choked out, "Good morning, J.T."

"See? Was that so hard?"

Her fingers curled tightly around the slender silver phone until she thought it just might shatter. Deliberately, she relaxed her grip while fighting down the urge to reach through the receiver and grab J.T.

"So, to what do I owe the dubious pleasure of having you track down my cell number?"

There was a long pause, and she'd almost convinced herself he'd hung up when he blurted, "Be at the palace by nine."

"What?" Her heartbeat skittered and she jumped to her feet, suddenly unable to sit still. Irritation forgotten in the swell of excitement peaking inside her, she waited, wanting him to repeat what he'd just said.

"I know you heard me."

Yes, she had. She just didn't quite believe it yet.

"I have the interview?"

"Ten minutes."

"*Ten* minutes?" It hadn't taken long to pop her balloon. She grabbed up her list of questions and knew it would take her longer than that just to read them aloud to herself. "It's not enough time."

"Nine minutes."

"J.T...."

"Eight."

"Fine," she snapped. "I'll take ten minutes."

"Good." He sighed into the phone, and Jade knew he wasn't happy about this. "Get here a little early. I can walk you through the protocol."

"I think I can handle it." As long as there wasn't a lot of curtsying involved. She did a lousy curtsy. Always had. Even in ballet class when she was a kid. At the end of a performance, she'd just bow along with the boys, rather than humiliate herself by getting her legs all tangled up.

"Probably," he agreed. "I'd still like to talk to you before you see Her Majesty."

That was reasonable, she thought. And hey, in

victory she could be gracious. "I'll be there at eight-thirty."

"See you then."

"J.T.—"

He hung up and a dial tone hummed in her ear.

Jade wasn't at all sure what she'd been about to say. She only knew that the abrupt conversation stung more than their arguments had.

"Cut it out, Jade," she muttered, and pushed the end button on her phone before tossing it back into her purse.

She sat down behind her desk again and told herself it didn't matter if J.T. was happy about this or not. It was her job. Her career. Her choice. She'd left J.T. for this world, so she had to succeed at it.

Otherwise, all that pain would have been for nothing.

Deliberately, she picked up her sheet of questions again and, forgetting all about her need for coffee, settled down to work.

She stepped out of the cab, and J.T.'s blood ran hot and thick in his veins.

Simple as that.

Jade Erickson stirred something inside him that had never eased up. He'd managed, for the last three years, to bury the passion and the need and the hunger for her. He'd told himself that he didn't care.

That he was over her. But it had taken only a day or two in her presence to bring it all back. Hard for a man to admit, even to himself, that he could be brought to his knees by a woman who'd already made it clear she didn't want him.

But as long as he kept that thought firmly in mind, he should be able to survive being with Jade—yet not being with her.

"Good morning." She looked at him and gave him a thousand-watt smile.

"You're pretty chipper," he noted, when he finally found his voice. "Nothing like getting your way to cheer you right up, huh?"

She actually winced, and he felt like an ass. Hell, it wasn't her fault his body was on full alert. Well, actually it was, but it wasn't like she was trying to do it.

Jade adjusted the strap of her black leather shoulder bag, then swung her hair back from her face. The wind had its own ideas, however, and twisted her soft, auburn hair into a wild halo that made his hands itch to touch it. Her forest-green jacket made her eyes glitter like emeralds. But unlike those cold, green stones, her eyes damn near glowed with an inner fire that warmed him even as it threatened to consume him.

But though she had him heated through, she

looked half-frozen. "In such a hurry you forgot your coat?"

"No, my assistant borrowed it and..." Her voice trailed off and a thoughtful expression flashed across her features.

"She didn't give it back?"

"I didn't even think about it until now, but no. Huh. She never brought me my coffee, either. That's strange."

"Yeah, a real mystery."

"So," Jade asked, shaking off her confusion. "Do I get to come inside, or will you be bringing the queen out here?"

"Right." He unlocked the iron gate that stood like a wall between them, and pulled it open, ushering her in. She smiled at the young soldier standing guard nearby, and J.T. noted the kid's near dumbstruck look. She carried quite a punch when she turned on the charm. J.T. almost felt sorry for the soldier. Almost.

"Come on, Jade," he said. "I'll get you some coffee."

She stopped and looked up at him. "As long as you didn't make it."

One dark eyebrow lifted. "I make good coffee."

"Yeah, if you're tarring a roof."

"Ouch." He'd argue the point, but why bother?

No one in the security office let him make coffee, either. "You're safe. Trust me."

He laid his hand at the small of her back and steered her toward the palace. Barely touching her, just the slightest brush of her jacket against his fingertips, he could still feel the electrical jolt of her nearness. But he cleared his mind of it. He wouldn't go back down that road.

They walked through the wide double doors and Jade stopped dead. Acres of marble stretched out in front of her and on either side. A wide, imposing staircase swung elegantly from the ground floor up to the second story. On the walls hung portraits of generations of kings and queens. A massive crystal chandelier dropped from the ceiling in the center of the entryway, and in the morning sunlight, hundreds of prism rainbows danced around the cavernous room.

She took a single step forward and did a slow, appreciative turn before letting her gaze drift back to J.T. "It's..."

"Big?" J.T. shoved both hands into his pockets to keep from reaching for her.

"Beautiful. And very fairy-taleish."

He smiled. "I don't think that's a word."

"It should be." She walked farther into the reception area and her high heels clicked against the gleaming marble floor. "I feel like I should be whispering or something."

"Not necessary," he said, though his own gaze did a quick sweep of the area. He worked here. He tended to take for granted the splendor that surrounded him every day. Not that he had the run of the place or anything, but even the public rooms in the palace were pretty damn impressive.

When he shifted his gaze back to Jade, he found her staring at him thoughtfully. "What?"

"Nothing." Jade couldn't have told him what she was thinking because she wasn't sure herself. All she knew was that he was even more stirring than this place. The grandeur of it all was enough to take anyone's breath away. But it had been too late in her case.

Just walking alongside J.T. was enough to do that.

"Okay then," he said, moving toward her. He caught her elbow in a firm grip and guided her across the floor toward a narrow hallway. "Let's get started."

Way ahead of you, she thought, and fought to ignore the heat streaming from the point of his touch right down to the soles of her feet.

Jade's stomach did a series of roller-coaster moves while her palms grew damp and her mouth went dry. She glanced at the clock on the wall of the security office where she sat waiting for J.T. He'd gone over protocol with her—no curtsying, thank God—and now she was just waiting for the go-ahead.

She was minutes from interviewing the queen of Penwyck.

"I think I'm gonna be sick," she muttered, then swallowed hard, hoping her stomach would cooperate and stay where it was supposed to.

What had she been thinking? Why had she pressed so hard for this? Who the hell was she to be interviewing a queen, for heaven's sake?

Jumping up from her chair, Jade paced to the window on the far wall. She looked out at yet another section of the gardens and wished she was out there, sprinting for the main gate and the street beyond. She'd been working toward this moment for three years. This one interview would push her over the top. Put her in a position to move forward in the career that had always meant so much to her. Now that the moment was here, she was terrified. And she wasn't sure what terrified her more, the idea of screwing it up or of succeeding.

"You ready?"

J.T.'s voice sounded behind her, and she turned to look at him. Those dark-brown eyes of his locked onto her and she felt the warmth of his stare ease away the last of the nerves rattling her insides.

"As I'll ever be." She stopped long enough to snatch up her purse from the corner of a desk, then walked out of the office, J.T. at her side.

"We'll have to take the service elevator," he was saying, and it took a moment or two for his words to register.

"But the stairs. The marble staircase—"

"Being polished as we speak." He guided her farther down the hallway. "No sweat, though. The service elevator's small, but it'll get us upstairs."

"Small." Jade's stomach did another weird dive, but she held it together. How bad could it be? One short elevator ride. No problem.

He came to a stop and punched a button. As a motor whirred, Jade tightened her grip on her purse, digging her fingernails into the pliable leather.

The door slid open, J.T. followed her inside and she turned around in time to watch the door slide closed again. Small, she thought. Too darn small. What's the matter with this place? They couldn't afford a bigger elevator for the employees? What was this, the Middle Ages?

Her heartbeat sounded like a bass drum.

The elevator shimmied, shuddered, then stopped with a jerk.

She stared at the closed door, willing it to open. One second passed. Then another.

"Why isn't the door opening?" A reasonable question, she told herself.

"I don't know." J.T. punched a couple of the buttons, and when nothing happened, he opened a panel on the wall and plucked a phone from its cradle.

His conversation was pitched low enough that Jade missed most of it, but chances were even if he'd been speaking in a normal voice, she wouldn't have heard him over the wild hammering of her heart. At last he hung up the phone and turned to look at her.

"Get comfortable," he said, clearly disgusted. "Power's out. Looks like we're stuck for a while."

"What?" She grabbed two fistfuls of his sweater. "Get me out of here, J.T. Now!"

Seven

"**W**e can't be stuck." She released her grip on his sweater, then pushed past him and pressed first one then another of the buttons on the narrow panel. "How can the power be out?" she mumbled, her fingers flying over the numbered buttons. "We can't be out of power. We're in the palace. They *own* the power." She shook her head, refusing to believe. "Palaces don't run out of power."

"The power's not off for the whole palace. Just the back end here. Somebody crossed a couple of wires that shouldn't have been crossed and…" He shrugged. No point in going into the clumsy details.

"Wires?" Stunned, she spared him a glance. "Well, why can't they uncross the stupid wires?"

"They blew something. Relax, Jade." J.T. watched her for a long minute and frowned as she repeatedly hit button after button, each stab stronger than the last. What the hell was going on here?

"I'm relaxed," she assured him, tossing him another quick look over her shoulder. "I'm just trying to fix this, that's all."

"We can't fix it from in here, babe." He lowered his voice instinctively. He'd never seen her like this before. The Jade he knew just wasn't the type to get frantic over a glitch.

Reaching out, J.T. caught her hands in his and turned her around to face him. Her green eyes looked wide and scared, and that hit him hard. He'd seen her furious and passionate and tender and hurt and even worried. But he'd never seen her scared before. So he did what came naturally to him. He pulled her up close and wrapped his arms around her. Smoothing his palms up and down her back, he felt the tension inside her coil even tighter as the seconds ticked past.

"Hey," he said, keeping his voice hushed and comforting, "what's the deal? There's nothing to worry about, Jade. We'll be out of here soon."

She buried her face in his chest, pressing her cheek against his thick, navy-blue sweater. She sucked in a deep breath and blew it out again. "How soon?"

"Maintenance says a couple hours, tops."

"Hours?" She drew her head back and stared up at him, clearly appalled. "Hours? For a couple of wires? No way. Uh-uh. I can't do it, J.T. I can't stay in here for two hours."

J.T. stroked her hair back from her face, and though he was trying to soothe her, he couldn't help enjoying the soft, silky feel of the strands brushing across his fingers. Her eyes, those cool, sea-green depths, looked stormy now, wild with a need that he couldn't ease and didn't understand. "What's going on, Jade? Talk to me."

"It's…" She broke free of his embrace and took a half step back. Her gaze shot around the enclosed space, darting over every inch of the richly paneled elevator as if searching for an escape route. When she didn't find one, she turned her gaze back to him. "I'm just a little…*claustrophobic.*"

Now it was his turn to be surprised.

"You never said—"

"It never came up."

"We were married," he said, torn between sympathy for her and irritation that she'd hidden this from him.

"We had a ground-floor apartment. It didn't seem important."

"Looks pretty important right now," he said, and reached for her again.

She forced a smile that didn't go anywhere near her eyes. "I'm okay. Usually. I mean, I can stand it for a quick ride if I have to."

"You should have told me before we got into the elevator."

"I said I'm okay for short rides." She laughed and the sound was high and unnatural. "It's hours in a tight space I'm not so good at."

"All of this for an interview."

Her eyes went even wider. "The interview. It's ruined. I don't believe this." Shaking her head, she shot an angry glare at the ceiling, but aimed her barb a lot higher. "Does somebody up there hate me or something?"

"Will you relax about the damn interview?" J.T.'s temper flared. He pushed both hands through his hair, telling himself to calm down. To remember she was scared. All she ever thought about was her job. Even in a panic, the first thing that came to her was worrying about the blasted interview.

Her eyes flashed and he saw the same anger churning inside him reflected there. J.T. remembered her temper well, and idly, he reached up and fingered the scar she'd given him on their honeymoon. She noted the action and ground her teeth together.

Claustrophobic panic forgotten in the surge of anger, she faced him down like an amazon. Swinging her hair back, she tossed her purse to the floor. Brushing the edges of her jacket back, she planted both hands on her hips and glared at him.

"Easy for you to say 'oh relax, Jade.' *You* didn't want me to succeed at this, anyway."

"I never said that."

"You didn't have to."

"Ahh…so you're a mind reader, too." J.T. nodded sagely and folded his arms across his chest. "Hell, no wonder the station wanted to send you for this job."

"That's very funny," she snapped. "But inaccurate. I didn't have to read your mind to know what you thought of my working, J.T. Don't you remember? You made yourself perfectly clear."

He *did* remember. All too well. Their fights, the arguments. She'd wanted a career, he'd wanted a wife. And they hadn't been able to compromise enough to see that maybe both were possible. He guessed that was what happened when two hard-headed people came together. No one wanted to give an inch.

"Fine. So shoot me. I loved you. I wanted to take care of you."

"You wanted to keep me quietly at home."

"Well, there's a crime."

"I didn't *say* it was a crime," she retorted with

a frustrated groan. "I only said it wasn't for me." Jade walked the three steps to the opposite wall, then came back again. "God, you never listen. Not then. Not now."

That stung. "I listened plenty." He grabbed her and yanked her close up against him until he could have sworn he felt her heart beating against his chest. She tipped her head back to stare up at him, and he damn near drowned in the sea of her eyes. Her scent invaded him, surrounded him, flooding him with sensations, memories, until he was choking with them. He forced himself to shove his reactions aside and say what he'd wanted to say for so long.

"That last morning. You said you couldn't be happy without a career. Said that marriage to me wasn't enough. That our family wouldn't be enough."

Her eyes filled, but she blinked back the tears, and he couldn't be sure if they were tears of frustration or anger or just plain misery.

"You said you needed to find your own way," he added. "To make your own choices and forge a career that would mean as much to you as mine did to me." He pulled her even tighter to him. "Remember?"

"Yes," she whispered, and her mouth worked as her teeth bit into her bottom lip.

"So now I want to know. You walked away. Was it worth it? Are you happy, Jade?"

Happy?

Right now, the only thing making Jade happy was his nearness. She felt the heat pouring from him and the brush of his breath across her cheeks. She stared up into the dark-brown eyes she'd been dreaming of for three long years and knew that she'd still be seeing them in her sleep if she lived to be ninety.

Happy?

Without J.T.?

Impossible.

But she couldn't tell him that. Couldn't tell him that so far, her career hadn't been enough to fill the emptiness he'd left behind. Couldn't admit that maybe, just maybe she'd been wrong to walk out.

"I have a good job."

"Are you happy?"

"I have a good life."

"Are you *happy*?"

His voice was a low growl of need, demanding an answer.

"Yes." She lied. Looked right at him and lied through her teeth. Because anything else would just be too hard. Telling the truth would only toss a sackful of salt into a wound that was still obviously gaping open, unhealed.

Three years apart and neither one of them had

moved on. And there was a small voice inside her whispering that she was glad. Glad he still cared. Glad he missed her as much as she missed him.

"You're lying," he said tightly, pulling her even closer and wrapping his arms around her with a vise-like strength that threatened to snuff out her breath. "I could always tell when you were lying, babe."

"You're wrong."

"You miss me."

"No."

"You want me."

"J.T.—"

"As much as I want you."

Her knees quivered, and deep down inside, she went damp and hot and needy. Breath shuddering from her lungs, she licked her lips and watched his gaze lock on her tongue. "J.T. don't do this...."

"I've never stopped wanting you," he said, clearly not listening again. "I dream about you, then wake up, hard for you."

Desire coiled low in her belly and sprang loose, sending shards of excitement spiraling throughout her body.

"I know those dreams," she whispered, and just admitting it out loud was a sort of freedom. She moved her hands up his arms, letting her fingers explore the muscles hidden beneath the bulky sweater he wore. Her breasts flattened against his chest, her nipples aching for his touch. She shifted slightly, pushing herself against his body, and felt the thick, hard strength of him.

Instantly, her blood boiled. Heat poured through her, swamping her in a sea of need so vast, so deep, there was no escape but through him.

"No more talking." A low, tight moan pushed through his lips as his right hand swept up her spine to the back of her neck. He held her, fingers spearing through her hair, as he lowered his head and took her mouth in a kiss so wild, so fierce, he stole her breath along with any reservations she might have had left.

He parted her lips and let his tongue seduce her. At the first wet, warm stroke, Jade gave herself up to the reality of the moment. If she didn't have him *now*, it'd kill her.

J.T. backed her up against the wall, his hands moving over her body, ripping her jacket off and tossing it aside. As his mouth taunted her, teased her, stoked her inner fire, his fingers moved clumsily, eagerly to the buttons of her pale-yellow silk shirt. She pushed her hands between their bodies to help him, and in seconds, that, too, hit the floor. She didn't care. Didn't care about anything but his touch. His fingers moving now over her skin. His callused palms scraping along her rib cage to cup her breasts, still trapped in her lacy bra. J.T.'s thumb and forefinger tweaked at her nipples, pulling, teasing, and her knees turned to butter. She couldn't stand up, but again he was there, bracing her with the solid strength of his body.

She reached for the hem of his sweater and scooped her hands beneath it, yanking his shirttail free of his khaki slacks. Then she was touching him, feeling the hard, muscled planes of his abdomen, his chest. She ran her palms across his flat nipples and felt him shudder. Power scuttled through her and she gloried in the knowledge that she alone could bring such a big man to his knees.

Sliding up, up, she dragged his sweater and the plain white T-shirt beneath it up and off, tearing it from him and throwing it in a heap atop her own clothes. His upper body bared to her, she ran her fingers over his tanned, well-defined chest, relishing the feel of him.

J.T. reached behind her back, quickly worked open the clasp of her bra, and when she let the lacy straps slide off her shoulders, he cupped her breasts again, scraping his thumbs across the rigid peaks of her nipples. Jade moaned and tipped her head back with a thunk against the oak paneling. When he bent to take first one nipple, then the other into his mouth, she groaned louder, barely able to muffle the sound of the pleasure roaring through her.

His tongue and teeth did magical things to her

body and she trembled with the force of need rippling through her. It had been so long. So terribly long since she'd felt such wonders.

"I need you, baby," he muttered against her skin, and goose bumps raced along her spine at the brush of his breath.

"Yes, J.T. Now. Please now."

He swept one hand down the length of her, grabbed a fistful of her skirt and yanked it up around her waist. Then with his left arm he lifted her, bracing her back against the wall as she wrapped her legs around his middle.

J.T.'s heartbeat thundered in his ears. Somewhere deep inside him there was a small, logical voice whispering that he was nuts. That they were in a palace elevator. That he could lose his job for this. Hell, he could probably be *shot* for this.

And he knew it would be worth it.

He ignored that voice and cupped her center. Even through the fragile silk of her panties, he felt her damp heat waiting for him, and nearly came undone. Her lips were puffy from his kiss. Her nipples poked at his chest, and every time she breathed, they rubbed against him, pushing him onward. As if he needed the encouragement.

Watching her, he kept his gaze locked with hers as he slipped his hand beneath the thin elastic at her upper thigh and slid one finger into her depths. She sighed and arched into his touch, moving against his hand, rocking her hips and pulling him closer, deeper. Which was just where he wanted to be. One finger moved within her, slowly, deeply, and then it was two fingers exploring her inner heat, diving deep, as his thumb worked the tiny bead of flesh at her core.

She trembled in his arms and tightened her legs around him. "Fill me, J.T.," she whispered brokenly. "I need to feel you inside me."

Throat tight, breathing labored, he pulled his hand free, then with a snap, broke the elastic on her panties. She sighed heavily and moved even closer to him, scraping her hands up and down his chest, over his shoulders, to score her fingernails along his back. He felt every touch, every caress, like a branding iron. She marked him, inside and out, staking her claim to his body, even if she didn't want his heart.

But for now, this was enough.

This was all.

Quickly, he freed himself and pushed himself home. Her eyes went wide and glazed with a heat and passion that fed his own until he felt as if he was burning up from within.

Her tight, damp heat surrounded him, welcomed him and held him where he belonged. J.T. rocked his hips and pushed her higher against the wall. Her slim, elegant legs locked around his middle and pulled him tighter, closer. Her head tipped back and he buried his mouth in the curve of her neck. Inhaling her scent, tasting her, he fed on the pulse point hammering against his lips, and gave himself over to the crashing need racing through him.

Again and again he pulled free and slammed home, and each time it was like the first time. The same magic, the same heat, the same need. Building, firing up until he was blind with the urgency of desire and deaf to anything outside the tiny world created in the circle of her arms.

Jade held on for dear life. Her short, trim nails dug into the flesh of his back. Her legs tightened around his hips. Her back ached each time he pushed himself higher, deeper, but she wouldn't—*couldn't*—stop him. It was as if they'd been building to this climax for years. Everything in her life came down to these stolen moments in a stalled elevator, and nothing else in the world mattered but what J.T. was doing to her body.

Blood blistering in her veins, her heartbeat pounding in her ears, she forced herself to keep her eyes open, to keep them locked on J.T.'s. She needed to see him when she reached her peak. And as they climbed, as the tension grew and tightened and coiled within, her breath shortened and the low, familiar tingling erupted.

''J.T.'' She choked out his name.

"That's it, baby," he urged, his hands gripping her hips, his fingers digging into her flesh. "Give it to me, honey. Give it all to me."

She shook her head, swallowed hard. Fighting desperately to keep satisfaction at bay, she muttered, "Not without you. This time, we have to find it together."

"Together," he said with a groan, and leaned in for a kiss. One brief touch of his lips to hers and he reared back, saying, "Now, babe."

She felt his surrender and let go of her own quickly shredding control. As he pulsed within her body, Jade rode the crest of a tidal wave of sensation that took her higher and higher until at last it exploded onto the shore and left her mind and heart and soul splintered in its wake.

Eight

In the basement, two men huddled around a mass of wires spilling from behind the wall. The tall man in uniform standing behind them glowered. "Well?" he demanded. "Can you fix it or not?"

One of the workmen chanced a quick scowl at their observer. "'Course we can fix it. Just take some time, is all."

"How much time?" the soldier asked.

A loud snap, followed by a series of blue-white sparks shooting into the air, interrupted them. When the scent of burned rubber filled the air, the workman sighed, knowing that a few more insulated wires had just bitten the dust. "Gonna be a while yet."

Disgusted, the soldier stomped off to make his report. Man. He didn't want to be around when J. T. Wainwright finally got out of that elevator. The man would be pissed off enough to shoot first and ask questions later.

"Hope they don't fix this thing anytime soon," J.T. murmured, his voice muffled against the base of her throat. "If the door opened this minute and the king was standing there, I don't think I'd have the strength to care."

Jade clung limply to him, knowing he was absolutely the only thing holding her onto the planet. Without his heavy body pressed to hers, she'd probably float, weightless, right up through the roof of the elevator and out into the open sky.

She'd never experienced anything like that. Not even when she and J.T. were together. Oh, the sex had always been fabulous for them. But today was in a category all by itself.

"I don't think I can move," she said softly.

"No problem. I like you just where you are."

So did she. With his body still locked within hers, she felt...complete, for the first time in three years. For the first time since leaving him.

He lifted his head and smiled at her. "How's your claustrophobia?"

She laughed shortly. "I think I'm cured."

"Just think of me as your friendly neighborhood doctor."

"You give great prescriptions."

He shifted slightly and she moaned, feeling him fill her again as his body thickened.

"I don't think we're finished with your cure."

"There's more?"

"Oh yeah," he said, and brought his mouth down to cover hers. There would always be more, he thought wildly as he took her mouth in a deep, fierce kiss that demanded as much as it took. For her, there would never be enough. She was as she'd always been—the one woman for him. It didn't seem to matter that what they'd once shared was gone.

All that mattered was now.

And right now, she was naked and ready for him. He moved, rocking his hips, pushing himself deeper, higher within her, until he wouldn't have been surprised to touch her heart. And still he wanted, needed more. He wanted to be so deeply imbedded in her that they would never be able to be separated again. And though his logical mind told him that was impossible, that there were too many obstacles still standing in their way, his heart didn't listen.

And his body didn't care.

As he took her mouth, his tongue exploring, caressing, he slipped one hand between their bodies until he'd found the juncture of her thighs. She gasped into his mouth when his thumb found that one most sensitive spot. Her hips lifted and she opened herself further, inviting him to touch, to stroke.

His fingers worked her and he felt each ripple of excitement, each purr of satisfaction as it hummed through her. She fed him. Fed his need, fed his hunger and fired his blood until he looked at her through a red haze that wouldn't lift. Tearing his mouth from hers, he watched as clouds settled over the sea green of her eyes. Clouds of passion that only he could create. She trembled again in his arms and whimpered desperately as the first of the tremors began to course through her.

"J.T.—J.T.—"

"It's okay, babe," he murmured. "Feel it. Just feel it, Jade. Let me take you there again."

"Only you, J.T." She moved against him, tipped her head back and moaned through gritted teeth as her climax slapped her hard. Her body shook with the force of it, and J.T. indulged himself, watching her eyes glaze, seeing her skin flush, feeling her body contract and pulse.

And as the last of it passed over her, he moved

within her, in a slow, erotic dance that kept her dangling from the precipice. He teased them both with long, languid strokes, feeling every inch of her as she took him inside.

"Again," she told him breathlessly. Wrapping her arms around his shoulders, she hung on and hitched her legs higher around his waist. "Take me again, J.T. Take me even higher."

A low growl erupted from his throat and he gave her what she wanted, what they both wanted. Rocking his body into and out of hers, he took them both on a wild, dizzying ride of sensation, and this time when they fell, he held her closely and cushioned her fall.

Passion was a great equalizer.

Two people wrapped up in each other saw nothing, heard nothing, felt nothing of the outside world. But once that passion was sated, everything came rushing back. Jade closed her eyes briefly and rested her forehead on his shoulder. Despite what they'd just shared, despite the amazing "rightness" of being with J.T., absolutely nothing had really changed.

"You okay?" he whispered, and his voice was a low rumble of sound in her ear.

"Yeah," she said, because it was easier than the truth.

He eased back from her and set her gently onto

her feet. Turning around, Jade bent down to scoop up her blouse. When she straightened, her gaze landed on something she hadn't noticed earlier.

"Oh, God."

"What?" He reached for her, one big hand coming down on her shoulder.

"Is that what I think it is?" she asked, lifting one hand to point.

He followed her gaze. His hand tightened, fingers digging into her shoulder. "Damn."

"I'll take that as a yes," she said, still staring at the security camera tucked discreetly into a corner of the ceiling. Quickly, Jade turned her back on the blasted thing and slipped into her bra, then her blouse, in record time. *Talk about locking the barn door after the horse is halfway to town.* She was worried about getting dressed in front of the camera when she'd already…oh, God.

Her fingers flew over the bone-colored buttons, but she still managed to shoot J.T. a quick look. "Please tell me that if the power to the elevator is out, the power to that camera is out, too."

He scowled thoughtfully as he pulled his T-shirt and sweater down over his head. Why was it that men could get put back together again so quickly? It didn't seem fair.

While she kept her back turned to the glass lens pointed at her, J.T. moved in for a closer look. A minute passed. She knew, because she was counting the seconds.

"It's okay," he said finally. "I mean, we're okay."

"How do you know?"

"Look."

Oh, she didn't want to turn around. Didn't want to look at the stupid camera and think about what exactly could be on a security tape. Would they show the thing at parties?

"Jade, will you just look?"

She whipped around to face him, still keeping her gaze from the camera.

"It's as dead as the elevator," he said. "No red light."

"You're sure?" *Please* be sure.

"I'm sure." He shoved one hand through his hair and, clearly disgusted, said, "But if it had been working, I wouldn't have noticed."

"Me, neither," she pointed out.

"Yeah, but then it's not your job to notice things, is it?"

"Not your fault. We were a little…distracted."

That one simple word hit him like a bullet. He snapped her a look that froze her to the bone. All trace of softness in his face was gone as if it had never been, and in its place, his features took on the hard, distant look of the professional soldier.

"Distracted?" he repeated. "Is that all we were?"

"J.T.—"

"I don't believe this. You're doing it again."

"I'm not *doing* anything."

"Yeah, you are. Hell, you're backing up so fast, I can almost see smoke lifting off your heels."

He could read her better than anyone ever had. Though at the moment, Jade thought, that fact was far from a comfort. She *was* backing up. Distancing herself. For both their sakes.

"This isn't the time to talk—"

"It's never the time, is it, Jade?"

"That's not fair."

"But it's accurate."

"Come on, J.T.—"

He shook his head in silent amazement. "I should have seen this coming."

"You're impossible."

"And you're a liar." He stepped up so close, so fast, he stole her breath and gave her just a half second of worry before she remembered that this was J.T. and he'd kill himself before ever hurting her. "This was more than a distraction. More than just sex, and you damn well know it, Jade."

His eyes blazed with a dark fire that sizzled her skin. She watched a muscle in his jaw twitch and knew he was grinding his back teeth together. Just as he had every time they'd had a fight. She threw things and he ground his teeth into powder. Theirs had been a brief, but colorful, marriage. And even after all these years, he still knew her better than anyone else in the world.

Yes, making love here with him was more. It had been everything. Everything she'd dreamed of and thought about for three long years. Her body was still humming, every nerve ending on red alert, and if he looked the slightest bit interested, she had no doubt that she'd slip right out of her clothes again for another go-round.

And the moment that dangerous thought scuttled through her mind, she pushed it right back out again.

"What do you want me to say?" she demanded, deciding quickly to fight fire with fire. Planting both hands in the center of his chest, she gave a shove, and though it was like trying to move a mountain on a skateboard, she made her point and he quit looming. "What is it you want to hear, J.T.? That I saw stars? Well, I did. That it was great? Of course it was." She paused. "But it doesn't change any-thing."

"Well, you haven't changed any either, babe."

Prickly now, she snapped, "What's that supposed to mean?"

"You're the same Jade you were three years ago." He moved in again with a quiet, stealthy grace that threatened even as it excited her. "You're not only lying to yourself about us, you're too big a coward to stick around long enough to find out if things could be different."

So much for excitement.

Instinctively, she struck out. Drawing her right foot back, she swung out and kicked him dead in the shin. He winced, but gave no other sign that she'd hurt him. And damn it, she wanted to hurt him as badly as his words had cut at her.

"I'm not a coward."

"You ran away from me—from us—three years ago."

"I left, I didn't run. There's a difference."

"Not much. Just speed."

Exasperated, she demanded, "You think I wanted to leave?"

"Jade, I learned a long time ago you don't do anything you don't want to do."

"You didn't give me a choice."

"There's always a choice, babe."

"And stop calling me babe."

"Changing the subject?" he asked, and though he drawled the words out slowly, casually, his rigid posture and fierce expression told her how he was really feeling. "Getting a little too close to home, am I?"

"You're such a jerk, J.T."

"Name calling." He clucked his tongue at her. "And not very inventive name calling for Ms. Penwyck TV."

She fumed silently and he read her correctly again.

Both eyebrows lifted and he glanced around the floor of the elevator. "Sorry, no dishes for you to pitch at me. But I'm sure if you kick me again, I might forget about the whole coward thing."

"I'm not a coward and you know it. I wasn't afraid of you, J.T."

"No, you were afraid to stay and give our marriage a shot."

"It wouldn't have worked."

"We'll never know, will we?"

"Yeah, we do. You wanted a wife. A mother for your kids."

"Well hell, shoot me now for being an insensitive toad!"

She stalked forward, forcing him to back up in the too-small elevator. Funny, the tiny space didn't seem to be bothering her at all anymore. Poking him in the chest with her index finger, she went on. "You wanted dinner on the table at six. You wanted me to be happy staying at home, and you couldn't understand when I said I wanted more."

"What is so wrong with a man wanting to take care of his wife? His family?"

"Nothing's wrong with it, J.T. What's so wrong about a wife wanting to help out? Take part in her family's future?"

He sucked in a gulp of air, then clamped his lips together. Again she watched him grind his teeth together, and while he was silent, she said, "What's the matter, J.T.? No smart comeback? No witty rejoinder?"

"Fine. I was hardheaded. Stubborn. So were you."

"And butting our heads together was getting us nowhere."

"We might have found a way," he said, and once again his voice was pitched to a low rumble that seemed to scrape along her spine, leaving a trail of goose bumps in its wake.

"And we might have just gone on hurting each other." Jade swallowed hard and took a step back from him. "I didn't want that anymore. For either of us."

J.T. pushed one hand through his hair and took a long moment to get control of a temper that was still too close to the surface. He hadn't meant to open up that old can of worms. But being with her again, feeling her pressed to him…listening to her hushed sighs…he hadn't been able to stop himself.

"This really is just like old times, isn't it?" he

asked with a harsh, brief laugh. "Mind-blowing sex and then a big fight."

"I don't want to fight with you anymore, J.T."

He looked at her then and temper faded to a pang of regret that seemed to ricochet around his chest, leaving him bruised and battered. Reaching out, he stroked his fingertips along her cheek before letting his hand fall back to his side.

Then he bent down, picked up her jacket and held it out to her. She took it, shoving her arms into the sleeves as if she were putting on a suit of armor. But she didn't need it. Old hurts, old pain had risen up between them and stood there, strong as a brick wall.

"Sex was never the problem with us, was it, babe?" he asked, bending down one more time to snatch up her torn panties from the floor. "It was the whole pesky problem of trying to live together that did us in, wasn't it?"

She looked up at him and he saw pain shimmering in her eyes. "I've missed you, J.T."

"Ah, baby, I've missed you, too." He pulled her close for a hug that felt too much like goodbye for him to be able to enjoy it. "That's the hell of it, Jade. I'll always miss you."

Whatever she might have said was lost as the elevator jerked, the motor hummed and they started moving again.

"Looks like they fixed the problem," he said unnecessarily.

Jade grabbed her panties from him and shoved them into her jacket pocket. Smoothing back her hair, she picked up her purse, slung the strap over her shoulder and looked up at J.T. "Do I look okay?"

"Beautiful. As always." But his eyes were shuttered now. The J.T. she'd been with just moments ago was gone again, leaving her with the security expert who didn't like reporters.

And Jade's heart ached.

Nine

When the door slid open, J.T. knew instantly that something was up. The young soldier waiting opposite the elevator looked up at him and snapped to attention.

"Sir. Mr. Vancour would like to see you in the queen's reception room, sir."

"Now?" J.T. took a grip on Jade's upper arm and held her in place when she would have moved away from him.

"Right away, sir." The soldier nodded at Jade. "Ms. Erickson is to come along."

This didn't make sense. J.T. checked his watch

and realized they'd been trapped inside the elevator for a little more than an hour. *Time flies when you're havin' fun.* The queen, like every other royal, spent most of her days keeping to a tight schedule. Though the public no doubt thought of the royal life as an indolent one, there were any number of demands on their time, from charitable events to political meetings. And that wasn't even including the everyday things involved in trying to have a family life.

Taking all of that into account, J.T. knew there was no way the queen would simply be sitting in her reception room waiting for Jade to be released from a stuck elevator. The interview would no doubt be rescheduled. The fact that they were being hurried along to a meeting that wouldn't take place told J.T. that something was definitely up.

"What's happening?" Jade asked as they started off down the richly carpeted hall.

"Not sure," J.T. admitted, but he kept a tight hold on her arm and wasn't entirely certain whether it was for her benefit or his own.

Their steps were muffled and yet seemed to echo along the hall. As she walked beside him, J.T. felt Jade's fascination with the private area of the palace very few people ever saw. Landscape paintings, portraits and the occasional tapestry dotted the cream-colored walls. Chairs and desks lined the hall, antiques of staggering age, yet they looked almost new, a mark of the centuries of care given them here in the palace. Soft pools of ivory light spilled from golden wall sconces and created pale puddles of brightness on the dark-red carpet. Heavy velvet drapes were pulled across windows, keeping the morning sun from damaging fragile fabrics.

The beauty surrounding him was something he took for granted. After three years of duty at the palace, he'd long since ceased to be impressed with the casual elegance of the place. To him, it was simply the royals' home. The home he'd sworn to defend. But now, seeing it through Jade's eyes, J.T. felt a swell of patriotic pride in his country's seat of power.

"It's beautiful," she whispered. He kept her moving, but she turned her head from side to side, taking it all in.

"Uh-huh. It's right down here. Second door."

Jade suddenly stopped beside him and brought him up short.

"What's wrong?"

She swallowed hard and gave him a sheepish look. "I just wanted a second to sort of catch my breath."

"Gonna run?" he asked, and regretted it the minute the words left his mouth. Nothing like beating a dead horse right into the ground.

"No." Jade straightened up and took a calming breath. She'd have a breakdown later. Right now, in front of J.T., she sure as heck wasn't going to appear nervous.

Nervous.

A weak word for what was whipping around inside her at the moment. She'd come to the palace to do an interview with her queen. Scary on its own. Then she'd been trapped in an elevator and had made wild crazy love with her ex-husband. Just your average day.

She glanced at the open doorway. Just beyond the threshold was everything she'd been working for, striving toward for three long years. And now a part of her didn't want to go in. How logical was that?

It had all come down to the next few minutes. Did she have what it took to make it?

She'd reached her point of no return.

"Let's go," he said, and extended his arm in an invitation for her to precede him.

"Right." Lifting her chin, she walked stiffly toward the open doorway on her left and tried not to think about the fact that she was about to meet the queen—while carrying her torn panties in her jacket pocket.

Oh, God.

The reception room, unlike the dimly lit hall, was bright and airy. Sheer linen drapes were pulled aside, allowing sunshine to pour through glistening window panes that overlooked the rose garden. Directly in front of the floor to ceiling windows sat two Queen Ann style chairs with a small round table between them. Atop the table was an ivory porcelain vase filled to bursting with roses of every possible color. Red, yellow, ivory, lavender, they spilled from the vase with an artful ease and filled the room with their sweet scent. A lovely, inlaid writing desk was on the right, its surface dotted with neat stacks of papers. Bookcases lined two of the walls and a marble hearth boasted a cheery and welcome fire.

Beauty surrounded her.

But the queen wasn't there.

Jade buried a sharp stab of disappointment and glanced at the older man walking toward them.

"Ms. Erickson, I'm Franklin Vancour, head of—"

"The RII," she finished for him. "Yes, I know."

He nodded.

Why was the head of palace security waiting to see her?

"Problem?" J.T. asked.

The older man sent him a quick look before turning his gaze back to Jade. "Her Majesty understands why you were unable to keep your appointment, Ms. Erickson—"

"Jade, please."

"Very well. And she's offered to reschedule."

"Thank you. But that doesn't explain what's going on. Why was I brought in here when the interview has been postponed?"

"It'll be easier to show you." With that, he walked across the room to a hand-carved teak cabinet and opened the doors, to reveal a wide-screen television. He pushed the power button.

Instantly, Vince Battle's face appeared on the screen. Holding a microphone, he gave his audience the "sincere" look he was so well known for and started talking. "The young woman, Janine Glass, was abducted this morning...."

Jade gasped and took a step closer. J.T. moved up close behind her.

Janine's photo appeared in the upper left corner of the screen as Battle kept talking.

"So far, the police have no leads in the mysterious disappearance of the woman, who is employed by PEN-TV as an editorial assistant to our own Jade Erickson. Ms. Erickson has recently been the recipient of several threatening letters. We will be covering this story as the investigation continues...."

Vince's face disappeared and an ad for dishwashing soap bounced across the screen. Franklin Vancour shut the set off midjingle and Jade was grateful. Her nerves were suddenly stretched to the breaking point and one bottle of dancing soap might be all that was required to send her screaming down the halls.

"The police would like you to go in and answer a few questions."

"Of course."

Janine. Missing.

Instantly, memories rushed through Jade's mind. Only that morning, Janine had borrowed her coat to make a coffee run. And Jade had been so distracted by her own problems, her own coming interview, she hadn't noticed that Janine had never returned.

"How could I not notice?" she muttered.

"Jade." J.T.'s voice sounded low, reassuring, worried. His hand came down on her shoulder and she instinctively turned toward him, lifting her gaze to his.

"It's my fault," she confessed.

"What are you talking about?"

"Janine. She—" Jade shook her head and pointed at the now dark television "—went out this morning for coffee. I wanted a mocha. She volunteered to go, but it was cold, so she wore my coat. That's why I didn't have it when I came here and—"

"I'll leave you two alone," Franklin said softly, and he left the room. Neither of them paid him the slightest attention.

"So stupid," she continued, moving out from under J.T.'s grasp and striding to the wide windows.

Once there, she stared out at the tranquil beauty below and knew it couldn't help the racing thoughts pushing through her mind. "I forgot all about the mocha. I talked to you and found out about the interview and everything else went right out of my mind. God, I was in such a hurry to get here, I left the station without my coat. Never even thought about it. Should have noticed that Janine didn't come back. Why didn't I *notice?*"

"You didn't do anything wrong, Jade."

She whirled around to face him. Her heart thudding against her rib cage, she fought the wild sense of panic skittering through her. "Of course I did. I was so wrapped up in my own stuff, so full of myself and my precious 'career' that Janine wasn't even a blip on my radar. I just never gave her another thought." Tears shimmered in her eyes and she brushed them away impatiently. "J.T., what kind of person does that make me?"

"Human," he insisted, and closed the distance between them in a few long strides. Grasping her shoulders firmly, he gave her a little shake, more to get her attention than anything else, and said, "Jade, there's no way you could expect this woman would be kidnapped."

"No, but she didn't come back. She should have, but she didn't." Jade lifted a shaky hand and scooped her hair out of her eyes. "She was wearing my coat—'' Her eyes went wide and scared. She sucked in a gulp of air that tasted cold and bitter. ''It was a mistake. God. Janine was a mistake. Whoever took her probably thought they were grabbing *me*.''

His heart twisted in his chest and the pain staggered him. J.T. tightened his grip on her, as if to prove to himself that she was here, with him and safe. *Threatening letters.* The reporter's voice echoed in his mind as he realized that she was right. Jade probably had been the target. It was just bad luck for her assistant that whoever grabbed her had been sucked in by a slight resemblance and a borrowed coat.

''What the hell is going on, Jade? What's this about threatening letters? How long have you been receiving them?''

''A few weeks...'' She shook her head and sighed with a weariness that seemed to come from her soul.

''Weeks? What did the police say about them?'' His voice deepened into the one he used to command troops and get instant acquiescence. ''You *did* go to the police with them?''

''Of course I went,'' she snapped. ''They said it was probably nothing. That this kind of person is usually too cowardly to actually approach the object of his...*affection*.'' She groaned tightly. ''But they were wrong, weren't they?''

He looked down at Jade and everything in him went still as stone. She was in danger. She'd been receiving threatening letters. Some nameless bastard had focused on Jade and only a borrowed coat had kept her safe.

Helplessness, an emotion he rarely experienced, roared to life inside him, and J.T.'s instinctive reaction was to go out and pummel something. There had to be a target for this anger, this frustration at knowing that she'd been in trouble and he hadn't known a thing about it.

Three years ago, he'd promised to love, to honor, to cherish her. Now she was on her own, with a major threat hovering over her. Damn it. How was a man supposed to live with that?

Staring down into her eyes, he saw worry and misery there, and anger churned inside him at the man who'd caused it. "We'll get to the bottom of this. I swear it. He won't bother you again."

"You don't know that."

"Oh yeah, I do." Carefully banked fury crackled inside him, and J.T. vowed silently to do whatever he had to do to make sure she was safe.

"I'm not worried about me, J.T. Janine's gone. How can we fix that?"

"Trust me," he muttered. Dropping one arm around her shoulders, he pulled her close. "Trust me."

* * *

After two hours at the police station, they grabbed a cab and went to Jade's apartment. J.T. refused to leave her side and Jade didn't ask him to. Fear curled in the pit of her stomach and sent out tiny flickers of awareness every few seconds. Her mouth dry, palms damp, she tried to tell herself that everything would work out. But even she didn't believe that.

She stared out the cab window at the passing cars, the pedestrians strolling along busy sidewalks. The sun darted in and out of steel-gray clouds, in between fitful spatters of rain.

Janine was out there…somewhere. Fear curled up in the pit of Jade's stomach and formed a heavy knot that felt as though it was weighing her whole body down. She slumped back against the worn, green vinyl seat, then braced herself as the cabbie took a hard right.

She fell against J.T. and he caught her to him before she could pull away. He felt big, strong…*safe*. And everything in her wanted to fold up against him. Because she wanted it so desperately and didn't have the right to expect that kind of comfort from him, she straightened up.

"How long have you been getting the letters?"

"A few weeks."

"And the video?"

Jade closed her eyes and pictured his face as he'd watched the video tape she'd given to the police only a few days ago. Pure, raw fury had chiseled J.T.'s familiar features into a mask of rage that had convinced more than one of the police officers to lecture J.T. not to take matters into his own hands.

"It was delivered to my apartment just the other day."

"Delivered."

"Yes."

"So this guy—whoever—knows where you live."

She drew in a long, shuddering breath and struggled to fight off a new set of chills snaking along her spine. "Yes."

"You're not staying there alone."

"J.T.—"

"I mean it, Jade." He wrapped both arms around her as if she were trying to escape him.

That so wasn't her plan. She didn't want to be alone any more than he wanted her to be. Alone, she'd have too much time to think. To worry about Janine. To wonder where she herself would be now if she'd gone for her own coffee.

Oh, God.

"Where'm I supposed to go? A hotel?" Where she didn't know anyone? At least at her apartment, she knew her neighbors. There was a doorman she could call on for help.

"Home with me."

She looked up at him and saw that he meant it. Those dark-brown eyes of his locked on to her with an intensity that stole what little breath she had left. Oh, she wanted to go with him so badly she ached with it. She wanted to wrap herself up in his strength and let the world slide away. At least for a while.

But going with him now would only complicate a mess they'd pushed way out of shape with that incident in the elevator. And it wouldn't be an answer to her problem, because it would be only temporary.

"J.T., that wouldn't solve anything."

"Maybe it doesn't have to." He squeezed her tightly, briefly. "Maybe I just need to have you where I know you're safe. I need to *keep* you safe."

And for tonight, she thought, that was enough.

Ten

The vultures were gathered outside her apartment building, despite the now heavy rain.

As the cab pulled up to the curb, dozens of reporters rushed forward. Cameras snapped, flashes popped like tiny lightning bolts, and radio, TV and tape recorder microphones jutted from the crowd like quills on a porcupine.

J.T. tossed a handful of bills at the driver, grabbed Jade's left arm and pushed the cab door open, taking out an overeager reporter. The man stumbled back, wincing, but someone else jumped into the fray, more than willing to take his fallen comrade's prime spot.

"Ms. Erickson, is it true—"

"How do you feel about your assistant—"

"Do you *know* your stalker?"

Rain plopped onto umbrellas and spattered on the sidewalk. Thunder rolled across the sky, drowning out most of the voices. But the rabid eyes, the eager curiosity came through loud and clear.

"Get out of the way," J.T. ordered, half dragging Jade from the cab. Pulling her in close to his side, he strong-armed the foolish few who didn't step aside.

"A comment, Ms. Erickson—"

"The public has a right to know—"

J.T. kept stalking forward and the fury on his face kept most of the reporters at a discreet distance. The doorman hustled forward and opened the door just before they reached it, and once they were inside, the uniformed man tugged it shut again. The noise level dropped abruptly and J.T. gave him a grateful nod.

"Thank you, Charles."

"Of course, Ms. Erickson. If there's anything you need…"

But J.T. was already moving.

"I live on the third floor," Jade muttered, automatically heading for the stairs.

"I know," he said, and countered her move by steering her toward the elevator. He stabbed the up button, and while they waited, looked down at her. Her beautiful eyes looked bruised, shadowed with a kind of misery he'd never seen there before, and his heart ached to ease it.

"Elevator," she mused. "I've lived here two years and I've never used it."

He forced a smile, because she looked as if she could use one. "I figure after today, elevators would be no problem."

"Or the least of my problems." Her eyes closed and she leaned toward him, resting her forehead on his chest. "Gosh, J.T. What are we going to do?"

We. One little word. And it had such an impact.

He glanced over her head toward Charles, who kept his back turned, offering them a bit of privacy. Beyond him, though, were the reporters, clamoring at the glass doors, focusing their cameras, hoping for a good shot that would feed their afternoon news programs—or grace the front page of their newspaper.

Behind J.T. the elevator door slid open with a soft sigh, and he steered her inside, punched the third-floor button and kept her hidden from view with his own body until the door closed again.

Alone, he tipped her chin up with his fingers and looked directly into her eyes. "What we're going to do is keep you safe and wait…while the cops do their job."

"Wait?" She took a half step back, sucked in a greedy gulp of air and let it out again in a shaky rush. "Waiting is the hard part. The I'm-useless-and-twiddling-my-thumbs part."

"It's called patience."

"Never one of my virtues."

"I remember."

The elevator door opened onto her floor and she stepped out, J.T. right behind her. She heard his footsteps and counted each one as a blessing. God, how had she lived for three years without being able to turn to him?

Rifling through her purse, she came up with her key ring and quickly opened all three locks. Locks? Oh, they'd been very useful. But for a borrowed coat, she would have been kidnapped off the street by the man she'd feared would break into her apartment.... Thoughts tumbled over each other in her mind, each demanding her attention, until her head pounded with a pain that nearly blinded her.

Pain, guilt, fear, fury all swirled inside her until she was a bubbling froth of emotions demanding to be released. She stumbled into the room, threw her purse at the sofa and watched as its contents spilled onto the cushions, then rolled to the floor. Burying her face in her hands, she felt the tears come, and couldn't stem them. She hadn't cried in so long it was as though a dam had burst somewhere inside her, and now that the floodgates had opened, there would be no stopping the deluge.

"I can't believe this," she sobbed.

"It wasn't your fault."

"I hate this, J.T."

"I know. I'd like to be out there, doing something. Tracking down the creep who's been sending you letters." He shoved one hand through his hair with a vicious swipe. "Letters. A stalker."

She shivered.

"A career, Jade. This career you wanted so badly is what got you this nutcase."

She shot him a searing look through narrowed eyes. "I don't need this right now, J.T."

"Yeah, I know. But here it is." He scraped one hand across his face and tried to wipe away the image of some faceless creep following Jade, peeping at her from the shadows, threatening her. Scaring her. And it burned him up so much, he just had to say it. "This damn career of yours—putting you out in the spotlight for every head case in the world to see—that's the problem here. If we'd stayed married…"

"What?" she demanded. "Crazies only go after famous people, J.T.? Is that it? Well, turn the news on once in a while and watch more than the sports scores. It's not just celebrities being hounded." Marching up to him, she jabbed her index finger at his chest. "If we'd stayed married and had kids and I'd stayed home just like you wanted me to, I could have picked up a stalker in the grocery store."

"Chances are less likely than—"

"It's all chance, isn't it?" Looking up at him, she silently dared him to argue. "This could have happened anytime, anywhere. Unless you were planning on locking me up in a closet and never letting me out of your sight."

"I never intended anything like that and you damn well know it, Jade."

"How do I know?" she asked, and gave him a shove that didn't make her feel any better when he didn't so much as budge. "All you could talk about was what it would be like—you going off to work, me waiting for you with a kiss when you came home."

"Is that so bad?"

"For some people, no," she darn near shouted, hoping to get through to him, finally. "For me, *yes.*"

He looked down at her and read the fierceness in her eyes. "Fine. Maybe I was stupid and stubborn."

"A breakthrough."

"I didn't mean to chase you off, Jade."

"And I didn't want to run," she muttered, turning away.

"But the point is, you *did*. You left rather than try to make it work."

"Oh, J.T. Do we really have to go through all of this again? Haven't we beaten this dead horse enough?"

The cold knot in his chest dissolved slightly. "Yeah. We have."

"For what it's worth," she said, turning her gaze on him and heating him through, "I'm glad you're here today."

"Good. Get used to me, because I'm not going anywhere."

It almost sounded like a threat. But Jade chose to take it as a promise. One for which she was immensely grateful. No matter what had happened between them three years ago, there wasn't a man alive she felt safer with than J.T.

She didn't know what she would have done without him the last few hours. A deep, bone-chilling cold had settled on her the moment she'd seen Janine's face on the television report, and it hadn't left her since. She couldn't get warm. No matter how long she rubbed her hands or leaned into J.T.'s bulk, the cold remained.

Janine had been kidnapped in *her* place. There was no getting around it. Even the police were convinced that Jade's stalker had finally come out of the woodwork only to make a mistake by grabbing the wrong woman. *She must be so scared. So frightened. And she, unlike Jade, was alone.*

"The police have some leads," J.T. reminded her. "Witnesses who saw a van idling in front of the station."

"Good," she said, and heard her voice break. "Can't be more than a few thousand vans on the island."

"They'll find her."

"In time? Will they find her in time? What is this guy gonna do when he realizes he grabbed the wrong woman?"

"I don't know. And neither do you, so stop imagining the worst."

"The worst is all I can think of, J.T."

She sensed more than heard him come up behind her. And when he turned her in his arms and pulled her close, Jade gave in to the need to cling. She wrapped her arms around his middle and hung on as if he was the last stable point in a whirling universe. And he was.

Everything that had been true and right in her life a few days ago no longer existed. Her comfort zone had been eradicated and there was no way to get it back. She'd fooled herself for three long years. She'd taught herself to believe that she didn't need J.T. Didn't want him. Didn't love him. She'd schooled herself in the belief that a career she'd built and forged for herself out of nothing would be enough to ease the loneliness that crawled through her during the long hours of the night. She'd fought her way nearly to the top of the heap, and now found it didn't mean anything. She'd worked hard, slept little and thought about nothing but her work for so long that only now was she realizing how small and insular her world had become.

Then, with a solid thump, reality had crashed down on her, slamming her back with a force that still staggered her hours later.

Facing those reporters, mirror images of herself, had hit her like a hard fist to the midsection. Their single-minded pursuit of the all-important "story" made them look like a pack of hungry wild dogs. They'd practically slavered over the chance to be the one to get her to speak.

They didn't care that her heart was wounded, that her mind was tortured by what-ifs. They didn't care that she was a real person, with wants and needs and fears. To them, she was only a story. A short piece on the evening news. Two columns in tomorrow's paper.

And Jade was suddenly sickened by the realization that she'd been doing everything in her power to become one of them.

"Oh, J.T.," she muttered thickly, tightening her grip on him until her arms ached nearly as much as her heart. "What was I thinking? How could I be like them? How can I keep on being like them?"

"You're not," he assured her, but she knew he was wrong. Felt it deep inside. And as if he sensed her doubts, he held her back from him so that he could look down into her eyes, convince her with the steely confidence gleaming in his own. "You're not like them, Jade. Yeah, you're a reporter. A good one, though it pains me to admit it." He smiled, and she wished to hell she could smile back. "But you still have a soul. A heart."

"Do I?" She pulled free and shoved both hands through her hair. "I'm not so sure."

"I am."

"How can you be?" She whirled around to challenge him. "I've badgered you for days just to get into the palace."

"Doing your job."

She laughed shortly, a harsh bark of disbelief. "Listen to you! How can you stand there and defend me when you've been doing everything you can to keep me out of the palace?"

"*My* job."

"This all went so wrong," she said, her voice reflecting the confusion blistering her mind. "I don't know how. But somehow, somewhere, I lost it."

"It?"

"My reason," she said, trying to explain something she still didn't quite get. "My reason for doing this. For starting this whole mess in the first place."

"Jade..."

"No." She shook her head fiercely, sending her hair into a flying wedge of auburn. "I have to figure it out. Have to know. Then I'll know how to fix it." She paced, her steps fast and muffled against the plush carpet. "My dad, but that's so politically correct. Blame it on your parents if you screw up your life."

"Jade, stop it."

"But you knew him. You saw how he was with me and my brothers. I wanted to prove to him that I was as good as the guys. Wanted him to look at me and know that I'd done something. Something well." She laughed again and the sound tore at J.T.

He'd watched her try to please her father, but even back then, he'd known it was useless. The old man would never be the kind of father she'd wanted, needed. Not because he didn't love her, but because he just couldn't understand her. Give him a rugby match or a night in a pub, and he was an affable man. Put him in a room with his daughter and he couldn't think of a thing to talk about.

"But it was more than that," she was saying, and J.T. paid attention, following her herky-jerky movements as she walked back and forth across the apartment. "I wanted it for myself." She looked up at him, and even across the short distance he saw guilt and remorse well in her eyes. "I wanted to prove to myself that I could make it to the top. And when I fell in love with you, I couldn't let you get in the way of that."

"I know." Old anger rose up inside him, but he tamped it back down. Hell, she was already being torn in two. He wouldn't add his pain to the burden staggering her. He took a step forward, but she stepped back, maintaining the distance and holding him at bay with one raised hand.

"I loved you, J.T. More than I've ever loved anyone or anything. But you scared the hell out of me."

"What?" Apparently, they were going to beat that dead horse just a little longer.

"You wanted me to be what I don't know how to be. What the heck do I know about being a mother, for God's sake?" She threw her hands wide and let them slap down against her thighs. Her bottom lip trembled, and he watched her deliberately calm herself. "And a wife? I don't remember much about my mother, but I do remember seeing her jumping up and waiting on my father like he was a king. She did what he asked, when he asked, to keep him from shouting, and as far as I know, she never had much of a life herself."

Damn it. Between the two of them, they'd managed to make a mess of things. Of course Jade had left him. Why would she stay when he seemed to be saying and doing all the things her father had?

J.T. had had three long years to regret past mistakes. Now he wondered if she, too, regretted what they'd lost. What they might have had. What they might have found, together.

"I got scared and I ran. From you. From *us*."

"Yeah, well, I made plenty of mistakes, too," he said softly, soothingly. He spoke as if he were trying to coax a frightened wild animal closer. "But it was a long time ago."

"Yeah," she agreed. "But here we are again. And I don't know what to do about that."

He took a step toward her and celebrated internally when she didn't back up. "Maybe we shouldn't worry about it right now."

She shuddered, a violent trembling that started at the top of her head and wracked her body all the way down to her feet. "J.T., I'm so tired of being alone. I—"

He reached her then and pulled her close, his heartbeat pounding in a rhythm to match hers. It killed him to watch such a strong woman torturing herself. To see tears in her eyes. To hear the shaking in her voice that she couldn't quite disguise.

"You're not alone, babe. Not now."

Reaching up, she cupped his face in her hands

and drew him down to her. "Don't leave me, J.T. Stay. Stay with me."

"I'm not goin' anywhere." Hell, he couldn't have been blasted from her side by mortar fire.

He kissed her, pouring his love, his fear, his worry into the act and nearly sending them both toppling to the carpet. But he caught himself in time.

Scooping her up into his arms, he muttered, "Bedroom?"

"There." She pointed and he started walking.

They were barely through the door when J.T. was setting her on her feet and helping her lose the clothes that were now so clearly in their way. Within seconds they were naked on the bed, and he rolled her onto her side, stroking her skin, relishing the feel of her smooth body beneath his hands. His insides lit up like a damn Christmas tree just to be holding her again, touching her again, and when he looked into her eyes, he saw the same desperate pleasure staring back at him.

He took her mouth in a deep, soul-satisfying kiss, and while he teased her lips, her tongue, he stroked her long, lean body until she trembled beneath him. Want and need and pain and love shimmered in the air around them.

Rain slashed at the window panes, beating out a rhythm designed for lovers. Wrapped in the warm cocoon of soft quilts, fresh sheets and the heat of dazzled flesh, they found each other again. Tomorrow or the next day, things might be different. Might change.

But for now, J.T. thought as he slid into her damp heat, this was all that mattered. She was all he'd ever really needed.

She arched into him, breathing his name. Her hands moved down his back, her fingernails scraping at his skin. He bent his head to kiss her as their bodies moved in an ancient dance, and with the first brush of her lips, he knew he'd found his home. The home he'd lost three years ago.

The home he might never find again.

The crashing pleasure of being a part of her and feeling her slip into his soul overwhelmed him, tearing at him. He linked his hands with hers, their fingers entwined, squeezing tightly. He moved and she shifted with him, silently urging him on, wanting him to take her higher and higher.

And when they took the plunge into oblivion, they made the leap together.

Eleven

A few hours later, Jade was settled in J.T.'s apartment on the palace grounds. While she napped, J.T. flopped onto the couch, picked up the television remote and stabbed the power button.

He flicked the channel to PEN-TV, turned the volume down and watched Barracuda Battle do a live report from outside the palace.

"Police are saying very little about today's abduction of Janine Glass, editorial assistant to our own Jade Erickson. Ms. Erickson has been unavailable for comment, but PEN-TV has discovered that she is now staying with Jeremy Wainwright, a high-ranking member of the RII.'' He waved a hand at the closed and locked palace gates behind him. ''Could this mean the palace has information about the abduction of Ms. Glass? For the moment, no one is saying.''

''My God.''

Jade's voice from behind him had J.T. shutting the TV off and tossing the remote onto the table in front of him. ''I didn't know you were awake.''

''Can't sleep.'' She rubbed her hands up and down her arms as if trying to ward off a chill. ''Did you hear him? Now he's making it sound like a national conspiracy.''

J.T. shrugged. ''He's a reporter.''

She looked at him. ''Don't think much of us, do you?''

''Necessary evil, I guess,'' he said.

''Like taxes?''

He gave her a half smile, but Jade hardly noticed. She started pacing, moving about his small living room, running the tips of her fingers across the glass fronts of the framed commendations lining the walls. J.T. just watched her. He'd tried to imagine her here before, but somehow he'd never been able to pull it off. He had one of the smallest of the bachelor quarters, but it suited his needs. If he and Jade had stayed married, they'd be living in one of the huge apartments set aside for high-ranking married officers.

Here, there was a tiny living room, a bedroom, a bath and a closet-size kitchen—not much to show for a man's life. The awards he'd received for doing his job were gathering dust, and when he went to bed at night, he went alone. He had a few close friends, but no family, except for his uncle Mike.

J.T. had expected his life to be different. He'd expected Jade to be in it. And seeing her here now, he tortured himself with thoughts of what might have been. But a few minutes of that were all he could take. Pushing himself up from the couch, he asked, "Want a drink?"

"What?" She half turned and looked at him blankly for a long second or two. "Oh. Okay."

He walked into the kitchen and felt more than heard her follow him. The room got smaller with every passing second and he told himself to ignore it. When this crisis was over, she'd go back to her world and leave him to his.

Reaching into the fridge, he pulled out two bottles of beer, twisted off the caps and handed her one. Then he shut the refrigerator and leaned back against it.

"Thanks." She took a drink, then studied the bottle between her cupped palms as if the label held the secrets of the universe.

J.T. took a couple of long swallows and waited. It didn't take long.

"You know," she said, keeping her gaze fixed on the damn beer bottle, "I never really thought about what it was like for the person on the other end of the story."

"Didn't you?"

"I know now what it's like to be the target of a hundred microphones. To have cameras pointed at you and questions shouted at you until you just want to scream." She set the beer down on the small table and dropped onto one of the two chairs. "What if the police don't catch this guy? What if they never find Janine? Then what?"

J.T. took a drink of his beer. "It's a small island, babe. They'll find her."

"Alive? Unhurt?" She leaned forward and cupped her face in her hands. "Either way, the world will go on, and the only people who'll remember will be me and Janine's family. To everyone else, this is just the latest story. The biggest splash. By next week, there'll be something different. Something fresh. Something new. And nothing will have changed."

But she had.

Jade felt the change right down to her soul. She'd worked so hard, planned so long to get to just this point in her life. Yet what did she have now that she'd reached it? She was suddenly the quarry rather than the reporter. A stalker was after her. Her assistant was missing. She couldn't stay in her own apartment because it wasn't safe.

So what was the point of any of it?

She'd gained a career that was suddenly becoming less and less important as the seconds ticked past—and in the process, she'd lost J.T. Being with him, making love with him again, had only served to remind her of just how much she'd given up when she'd walked out of his life.

And she wasn't sure she'd be able to walk away again. Even if she wanted to.

The next couple of days, J.T. kept Jade close by. Until the police found the man they were looking for, he wanted Jade where he could protect her. And the palace was the one place he knew was secure. No one would be getting to her here.

Of course, living with her again wiped away the misery of the last three lonely years. It all came back, what they'd had together, and he nearly choked with the sweetness of being able to reach out for her in the middle of the night. He held her while she slept, made love with her every chance he got, and called himself all kinds of a fool in his more lucid moments.

He was kidding himself.

He knew damn well this was temporary. Jade would no more stay with him when this was over than she had three years ago. In a crisis situation, people clung together. Once the crisis was past, they drifted apart again.

It tore at him, knowing that soon she'd be gone and his apartment would once again only echo with memories. But at the same time, he told himself it was better this way. Better to lose her outright than to let her all the way back into his heart, only to have her walk out again when things got tough.

Right now, she was torturing herself with guilt and misery over Janine. But when the woman was found, when this was all done and finished, then what? Jade hadn't been the homebody sort three years ago, and that hadn't changed.

"Anything from the police?" Franklin Vancour stepped up behind him as J.T. kept a wary eye on the reporters still camped outside the palace gates.

"Nothing," he said without turning around. "They're still saying they're following leads. But it's been nearly three days."

"Yeah, and the sharks are still circling."

J.T. nodded. Even as he stood there and watched, a couple of reporters tried to interview the gate guards. Naturally, the professional soldiers wouldn't even look at them.

"On the bright side..."

J.T. snorted. "There's a bright side?"

"With every reporter in the country focusing on

your ex-wife and the missing woman, no one's asking questions about the king.''

Well, that wasn't completely true. At this very moment, one reporter was finally getting that interview she'd wanted so badly.

J.T. turned and glanced at the palace. "*Almost* no one."

Jade sat stiffly on the edge of a Louis XVI chair and tried not to let her nerves show. Strange, all she'd been thinking about for a week was getting this interview. And now that it was here, it was almost anticlimactic. And so unimportant in the grand scheme of things.

With Janine still missing, Jade could hardly bring herself to care about something as trivial as a royal interview.

She jumped to her feet at the thought and walked toward the wall of windows overlooking the rose garden. From the vase on the table came the combined scents of fresh roses, perfuming the air until it was almost too thick to breathe. The sweetness seemed cloying, and Jade wished to heaven she could just open one of the windows. Take a deep breath. Clear her head. Try to remember why it had been so damned important to get to this one moment in time.

A scuffling sound beyond the nearly closed door

on her right caught her attention, and she moved a little closer. Frowning to herself, she heard a woman speaking, and in the next instant recognized that voice as the queen's.

"I assure you I've investigated the facts myself," the queen was saying—to whom, Jade had no idea. "There is no mistake. My brother was involved with the Black Knights and part of their plan to kidnap my husband."

A moment later, the queen lowered her voice. There was a hushed response and then a second or two of silence. Jade used that extra moment to slip quietly away from the door and retake her seat on the uncomfortable, but beautiful, chair.

Her brain spun with the impact of what she'd overheard. The king? A kidnapping plot? Had his illness all been a ploy to throw reporters and the public off the real story? And what was she supposed to do about this now that she knew?

That decision was postponed when the queen entered the room. Instantly, Jade rose, forced a smile and did a quick dip of her knee. "Your Majesty."

"Good afternoon, Ms. Erickson," the other woman said, as she stepped forward with her hand outstretched. "How lovely that we finally have the opportunity to talk." She checked a slim, gold watch on her left wrist. "I'm afraid I can only spare you

five minutes, though. There are a few pressing matters...."

"I understand," Jade said, wondering exactly
what those "pressing matters" might be. "And I
appreciate your time." She waited until the queen
was seated before taking a chair close by—and she
couldn't help wishing her cameraman was here. An
extra pair of eyes would have been helpful right
now.

"Your Majesty, everyone has been concerned
with the king's health."

The queen straightened her shoulders, lifted her
chin slightly and said, "The king is doing well. He's
being cared for by excellent doctors and has received a fine prognosis. There is no reason for concern."

Then why, Jade wondered, was there a flash of
worry in the queen's eyes?

"Can you tell me why there's been a virtual
blackout of the press? The palace has been refusing
to speak with us for weeks now."

"I'm sure you understand that with the king ill,
other matters have taken precedence over interviews."

It all sounded completely rational. And yet, as the
minutes flew past, Jade was more convinced than
ever that there was more to this situation than met
the eye. The queen was nervous. Though she was

gracious as always, her eyes shifted uneasily, and she seemed to consider every word before she spoke it.

Every instinct Jade possessed demanded that she tell the queen what she'd overheard, and ask for an explanation. But at the same time, she hesitated. Was it right to use something she hadn't been meant to hear? A corner of her brain scoffed at her for that. Of course it wasn't right, but it was what reporters did. They dug for dirt. Poked around until they found a weak spot and then reported it, not caring whether it did further damage or not.

And that, she thought, as the interview wound to its conclusion, was what separated her from the rest of the people in her profession.

She just didn't have that sharklike nature.

The question was…did she want to develop it?

A few minutes later, Jade left the queen's reception room with a notepad filled with quotes and a heart filled with confusion. She'd finally done it. She had the interview she'd been striving for, and now she stood in the empty hall and waited for the feeling of triumph to hit her.

But it didn't come.

This was the one thing she'd wanted, needed, to make the career she'd worked so hard for everything she'd planned it to be. There should be a sense of celebration. Victory. *Something.*

"But no—all I have is more questions." The interview was one thing. What she'd overheard was something else again.

She didn't know what to do. As a reporter, this might be the lead of a lifetime. The queen's own brother involved in a plot against the king? It sounded like a bad eighteenth-century novel. Every reporter clustered around the palace gate would sell their own mother to have this little nugget of information.

Yet Jade's indecision deepened by the minute. Her reporter's instincts told her to find a way to get this news out. To make a call to the station. Or at the very least, get access to a computer and start doing research on the queen's brother, the Black Knights and anything else she could find to add color to an already incredible story.

Walking down the long hall toward the marble stairs leading to the lower reception area, Jade's gaze passed over the portraits lining the walls. Centuries of Penwyck rulers glared down at her as if trying to intimidate her. And damn it, she did feel intimidated. She'd happened onto a private conversation. Did that give her the right to exploit what was obviously a painful family situation?

Her heels smacked against the marble steps as she

took them slowly, thoughtfully. Her right hand resting on the polished walnut banister, she let it glide along the cool, intricately carved wood and tried to imagine herself as one of the royals. They lived here. This was their home. In which she was a guest.

Here behind these walls, they strived to remain a family despite the pressure brought to bear on them by a country that demanded to know their every little secret. Triumphs and tragedies were reported and splashed across newspaper pages. Television cameras caught every misstep. And still there were the small secrets that every family had. Jealousies, heartbreak, celebration. These belonged here, in the palace. These were things that no one had the right to intrude on.

At the bottom of the stairs, Jade paused just long enough to glance out the front windows at the mob of reporters still clustered just beyond the gates. If she stepped outside, the shouts would begin and cameras would flash. Gritting her teeth, she turned her back on the others of her kind and hurried along the passage to the back of the palace, where she could escape into J.T.'s apartment.

"Ma'am." One of the soldiers posted in the reception area nodded to her as she passed.

How did they do it? she wondered. How did the royals put up with every little privacy being infringed upon? How did they smile when they wanted to scream?

And how could she be a part of causing the royals even more misery at a time when they surely didn't need it?

A brisk, cold wind lifted Jade's hair and sent a shiver along her spine as she left the palace and hurried across the open yard toward the apartment. Autumn leaves swirled and danced along her path, keeping time with her as she all but ran to the safety and warmth she'd found in J.T.'s place.

Stepping inside, she walked directly to the small, banked fire on the hearth and stood in front of it, letting the heat stretch out long fingers toward her. Then, leaning forward, she rested both hands on the narrow mantel and stared into the small, oval mirror above it.

Cheeks rosy from the wind, hair tousled and eyes troubled, she stared at her reflection and said, ''A week ago, you wouldn't have hesitated. You'd have run to the station with this.'' And it shamed her a little to admit it.

But now there was so much more to consider. She wasn't just a reporter. She was also a citizen of Penwyck. And she certainly didn't want to report anything that might endanger the king's life. But that wasn't all. There was J.T. to consider, too.

She drew back and stared around the room at the

citations for valor and loyalty lining the walls. He'd brought her here to protect her. To care for her. He'd trusted her. And if she used information that she'd picked up because J.T. had given her a safe haven, what would that make her?

The front door opened and J.T. walked in as if Jade thinking about him had conjured him out of thin air. She turned to face him, and read questions in his eyes.

"So you got your interview at last."

"Yeah." And so much more, she thought. Too much more.

One corner of his mouth lifted briefly. "I would have thought you'd be happier. You've been aimed at this for days."

"I know...." Jade pushed one hand through her hair and wondered how to tell him. She had to tell him. Right?

"Get everything you needed?"

"Oh, you could say that." God, maybe she shouldn't say anything, should keep it to herself. But then, not talking to each other was what had broken them up three years ago. Hadn't she learned anything?

He stepped into the room, closing the door behind him. "What's going on, Jade? What aren't you saying?"

Before she could answer, the phone rang, and

Jade wasn't sure if she was grateful or upset by the interruption.

J.T. walked to the phone and snatched up the receiver. "Wainwright."

She moved away from him, not even listening to his half of the conversation. Her head hurt with the thoughts rushing through it, and all she wanted to do now was talk to him about everything. Silently, she willed him to get off the darn phone.

A minute or two later, he hung up, and Jade turned to look at him.

"That was the police."

Police. Good God. What kind of person was she to have forgotten, even for a few minutes, about the woman who'd been kidnapped in her place? Jade took a step closer and held her breath. "Janine?"

"She's safe."

That breath rushed out of her in a sigh of relief.

He shoved his hands into his pockets. "Your stalker turned her loose about two hours ago. Seems she talked her way into his good graces. Convinced him to let her go."

Jade's heartbeat quickened and her knees felt weak. "That's Janine," she said with a shaky smile.

"Thanks to her description of where she was held, the police picked the guy up just a few minutes ago." J.T. stepped up close, dropped both hands on her shoulders and said, "It's over. You're safe."

"Safe." A good word, she thought. A wonderful word.

"Yeah. So, I guess you'll be going back to your own place now. Going home."

Home.

Great idea. The only problem was, she didn't know anymore exactly where home was.

Twelve

Relieved the Glass woman had been released unharmed, and more especially that Jade was no longer in danger, J.T. felt his chest tighten. With the threat to her over, he knew she'd be leaving. Going back to the world she usually lived in. The world that didn't include him. It was time to say goodbye to Jade again. And this time, "goodbye" was going to kill him.

Three years ago, his pride had been kicked, and when he'd lost her, he'd told himself that it was for the best. That they hadn't been in tune with each other's wants or needs. He'd tried to ease the misery by telling himself that he'd find someone else.

But he'd learned the hard way that there was no one for him but Jade. That was the simple truth. He wouldn't settle for second-best, and if he couldn't have the woman he loved, then he was looking at another thirty or forty years of loneliness.

And damned if he'd give in to that without a fight.

He wanted to grab her and hold on tight. To avoid doing so, he jammed his hands into his pockets. "Look, Jade," he began.

"J.T., I have to tell you—" she said at the same time.

Confusion and worry glittered in her eyes, and something cold and hard settled in the pit of J.T.'s stomach. No, damn it. He wouldn't give in this time. Not without a fight.

"You're not saying goodbye to me."

"I—" She cocked her head and stared up at him. "What?"

"Goodbye," he repeated, jerking his hands from his pockets to rake viciously through his hair. "We're not doing this again."

"This isn't about goodbye, J.T."

A brief reprieve. Fine. He'd take it. But they would talk about this. He wouldn't watch her walk out of his life again. "Then what?"

She lifted one hand to her mouth, nibbled gently at her thumbnail, then caught herself and stopped.

She gave him a brief glance, then deliberately shifted her gaze to one side.

Jade pulled in a long, deep breath and blew it out in a rush before saying, "Just before my interview with the queen…I, uh, overheard something at the palace I wasn't supposed to."

All right. This, he hadn't been expecting. And the fact that she wouldn't look at him wasn't a good sign. Instantly, his security instincts went on full alert. He folded his arms across his chest and waited. "Go on."

"The door to the reception room was partially open. The queen was talking to someone." She shook her head. "I couldn't see who. Guess it doesn't really matter *who,* does it? I mean, the point is really what I heard, not who she was talking to and—"

"Jade…"

"Right." Another deep breath. "She was whispering, really, in a hurried sort of way, and she said her brother had been involved in a plot with the Black Knights to kidnap the king."

There. It was out. Jade felt better already. At least now everything was out in the open.

Then she looked up at him.

His features had turned to stone. But his eyes flashed with a dark fire that reached across the room to singe her. If she didn't know him better, she'd already be backing up. Geez. As a professional soldier, he wouldn't even need a weapon to attack the enemy. Just that glare would be enough.

He tore his gaze from hers, shot a quick glance at the telephone, then turned that steel-melting stare back on her. "Who've you told? Who'd you call before I came in?"

"Oh, that's very nice."

"Who?"

Insulted, she straightened up and lifted her chin. "No one."

"Right." He snorted a harsh, mocking laugh as he stalked toward her. "You expect me to believe that you didn't jump on the biggest story of the year?"

He grabbed the phone, punched in two numbers and practically snarled, "Security."

"What're you going to do?" she demanded. "Arrest me?"

J.T. spared her another quick, disgusted glance, accompanied by the closest thing to a growl she'd heard in a long time. "Not hardly. But I am going to alert the palace press corps. Their spin guys can handle whatever you set in motion."

Stung to her heart, she simply watched him for a long minute. How could he think that of her? After what they'd been to each other, didn't he know her better than that? Didn't he trust her at all? And

if he didn't, could there ever be anything between them?

"You really think I'd do that?" She walked
around him until she was looking directly into his
eyes. What she read in his dark-brown gaze didn't
make her feel any better. He stared at her as if she
was some sort of bug under a microscope. Fasci-
nating, but just gross enough to demand squishing.

Jade reached out, grabbed the receiver from him
and slammed it down into its cradle. "I didn't tell
anyone," she said, willing him to believe her.

He looked at her, studying her eyes, but at least
he didn't grab the phone again. "Fine. You didn't
tell anyone. Yet, you mean."

Fury pounded through J.T. Fury directed at himself, not Jade. He'd known it was risky, having her
stay here at the palace with him. There were too
many secrets flying around the place. She was bound
to stumble across one or two of them. And now that
she had, he didn't know what to do about it.

God, what an idiot he was. He'd thought they'd
reconnected over the last week. He'd been about to
ask her to stay with him. To marry him again.

Idiot.

He glanced at her. Sometime during the last few
minutes, she'd snatched up her purse and slung it
over her shoulder. Ready to walk.

Perfect.

"I can't believe you don't trust me," she said.

"Why the hell should I?" He waved one hand at her. "Look at you. You're ready to hustle out the door already. Besides, all you've been talking about is getting a scoop. Now you stumble onto the best-kept secret in the palace and I'm supposed to just trust you not to say anything?"

She took off her purse and threw it onto the sofa behind her. "Yes." She planted both hands on her hips and glared at him.

"Right." Damn it, he wanted to trust her. Wanted to believe her.

"I could have reported it," she was saying, and threw both hands into the air as if reaching for the reason she hadn't. "God knows I thought about it. For a couple of seconds there, I imagined making the call, writing the story up and delivering it on camera. But I didn't—couldn't do it."

"Why?" He grabbed her upper arms and dragged her close. He studied her eyes, looking for the truth. And he found it. He knew those eyes too well for her to fool him. She hadn't told anyone, but that didn't explain anything. He had to know what was behind the change of heart. Why she'd turned her back on the very thing she'd left him for three years ago. "Why wouldn't you tell, when this is the one thing that could have cemented the damn career you wanted so badly?"

"Maybe...I've changed."

"Changed. After hustling me for a week trying to get a story."

"Is it so hard to believe?"

"Yeah." It was, though a part of him wanted more than anything to believe.

She actually winced. "Well, that's honest."

"Why?" One word, pushed past the strangled feeling in his throat. He pulled her even closer, until her breasts pushed against his chest. Until every breath he took drew her light flowery scent deep inside him. Until he felt the pounding of her heart and knew the quick, staccato beat matched his own. And still she wasn't close enough. "Why would you change now? What makes today different than a week ago?"

Her breath came fast and hard. Her pulse beat pounded at the base of her throat. J.T. buried the impulse to taste her there, and held his breath when she started talking. "Three years ago, I walked out when things got tough. Rather than stay and fight for us, I ran. But I'm not that girl anymore, J.T. I grew up—a lot of it this past week. And I finally know that there are some things more important than a story. Than my career."

"Like what?" He wanted—needed—to hear what he hoped she was about to say. His fingers tightened.

She yanked free of his grip, gave his chest a shove

that didn't budge him an inch, then snapped, "Like you, you big jerk."

Pacing wildly, Jade muttered to herself as she walked, shaking her head, swinging her arms high and letting them slap against her sides. "Unbelievable. He doesn't get it. He's never gotten it and nothing's changed. I love him, and still he doesn't believe me. I can't do this anymore, I swear. It's ridiculous to keep going over the same territory again and again and getting nowhere."

"Can I say something or is this a private moment?" J.T. asked.

"I wasn't talking to you," she snapped.

"You said you love me."

"I'm a slow learner."

"I love you back."

She stopped dead and glared at him.

"How can you love me and think I'd do something like betray your trust?"

"Three years ago, you walked away from us to have the career that story would have skyrocketed."

"Three years ago, you let me leave." Jade stared at him as she remembered. "Fear drove me then, J.T. Fear of the future, fear of the unknown and my own doubts. Yes, I ran. But you let me go, J.T."

He reached up and rubbed the back of his neck viciously. "I know."

"I thought you didn't care. Certainly not enough

to come after me.'' She shook her head, paying no attention to the tears beginning to course down her cheeks. ''So I couldn't go home again—even when, later, a huge part of me wanted nothing more than that.''

God, the time they'd lost, he thought, and all through stubbornness.

''You're right,'' he said, each word bitten off as if it carried a bitter taste. ''I pushed you away, and when you finally took off, I let you go because my pride was hurt. Hell, Jade, it was all I had left, so I clung to it rather than go chasing after you.''

''And now?'' she asked, needing to know.

''Now, there's only you.'' He looked into her eyes and wondered how he'd survived the last three years without being able to lose himself in those depths. ''Pride doesn't mean squat if I lose you again. There's no way I'm letting you walk away from me this time, Jade.''

That voice of his scraped along her nerve endings and she shivered. But he wasn't finished.

''Three years ago, I let my pride do my thinking.'' He walked across the room toward her, one slow, deliberate step at a time. ''When you left, it damn near killed me, but I didn't want you to know it. So I buried the hurt and told myself to get over it.''

''Did you get over it?''

He shook his head. "Nope." Another long step, and she swore she could almost feel the heat of him drawing closer. "There's no getting over you, Jade."

Her breath caught and her heart gave a quick flutter.

"And I'm through trying."

She inhaled sharply, deeply.

"If you run again, I'll be right on your heels."

"I won't run," she promised, looking up into those dark-brown eyes where she could suddenly see her future shining brightly. "I'm not a kid anymore, J.T. I'm willing to fight for what I want."

"And what do you want, Jade?" He stopped right in front of her, lifted one hand and trailed his fingertips along her jaw. Heat erupted between them.

"You, J.T. It's always been you."

He smiled, a slow, wicked smile that quickened a flame of expectation deep within her. Curling his fingers beneath her chin, he tilted her head back until their gazes were locked.

"Marry me again, Jade."

"When?"

"Now."

She laughed. "Now?"

"Okay," he hedged. "Honeymoon now. Wedding tomorrow."

"Now that sounds like a plan!"

She went up on her toes, wrapped her arms around his neck and hung on. J.T.'s arms came around her and lifted her right off her feet. He bent his head to kiss her, and when his lips came down on hers, Jade gave herself up to the sensation of sliding into the heaven only she and J.T. together could create.

* * * * *

Be sure to continue
the CROWN & GLORY *saga*
next month with
TAMING THE PRINCE
by Elizabeth Bevarly (SD #1474),
coming from Silhouette Desire.

**Where royalty and romance
go hand in hand...**

The series finishes in

with these unforgettable love stories:

THE ROYAL TREATMENT
by Maureen Child
October 2002 (SD #1468)

TAMING THE PRINCE
by Elizabeth Bevarly
November 2002 (SD #1474)

ROYALLY PREGNANT
by Barbara McCauley
December 2002 (SD #1480)

Available at your favorite retail outlet.

Silhouette Desire

presents

DYNASTIES: THE CONNELLYS

A brand-new miniseries about the Connellys of Chicago,
a wealthy, powerful American family tied by blood to the
royal family of the island kingdom of Altaria.
They're wealthy, powerful and rocked by
scandal, betrayal…and passion!

Look for a whole year of glamorous and
utterly romantic tales in 2002:

Silhouette®
Where love comes alive™

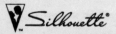

Silhouette®

Desire®

**Meet three sexy-as-all-get-out cowboys
in Sara Orwig's new Texas crossline miniseries**

STALLION PASS

These rugged bachelors may have given up on
love…but love hasn't given up on them!

Don't miss this steamy roundup of Texan tales!

DO YOU TAKE THIS ENEMY?
November 2002 (SD #1476)

ONE TOUGH COWBOY
December 2002 (IM #1192)

THE RANCHER, THE BABY & THE NANNY
January 2003 (SD #1486)

Available at your favorite retail outlet.

Silhouette®

Where love comes alive™

October 2002
TAMING THE OUTLAW
#1465 by Cindy Gerard

Don't miss bestselling author
Cindy Gerard's exciting story about
a sexy cowboy's reunion with his
old flame—and the daughter he
didn't know he had!

November 2002
ALL IN THE GAME
#1471 by Barbara Boswell

In the latest tale by beloved
Desire author Barbara Boswell,
a feisty beauty joins her twin as a
reality game show contestant in an
island paradise…and comes face-to-
face with her teenage crush!

December 2002
A COWBOY & A GENTLEMAN
#1477 by Ann Major

Sparks fly when two fiery Texans are
brought together by matchmaking
relatives, in this dynamic story by
the ever-popular Ann Major.

MAN OF THE MONTH

Some men are made for lovin'—and you're sure to love
these three upcoming men of the month!

Available at your favorite retail outlet.

Silhouette®

Where love comes alive™

COMING NEXT MONTH

#1471 All in the Game—Barbara Boswell
She had come to an island paradise as a reality game show contestant. But Shannen Cullen hadn't expected to come face-to-face with the man who had broken her heart nine years ago. Sexy Tynan Howe was back, and wreaking havoc on Shannen's emotions. She was falling in love with him all over again, but could she trust him?

#1472 Expecting...and in Danger—Eileen Wilks
Dynasties: The Connellys
They had been lovers—for a night. Now, five months later, Charlotte Masters was pregnant and on the run. When Rafe Connelly found her, he proposed a marriage of convenience. Because she was wary of her handsome protector, she refused, yet nothing could have prepared her for the healing—and passion—that awaited her in his embrace....

#1473 Delaney's Desert Sheikh—Brenda Jackson
Sheikh Jamal Ari Yasir had come to his friend's cabin for some rest and relaxation. But his plans were turned upside down when sassy Delaney Westmoreland arrived. Though they agreed to stay out of each other's way, they eventually gave in to their undeniable attraction. Yet when his vacation ended, would Jamal do his duty and marry the woman his family had chosen, or would he follow his heart?

#1474 Taming the Prince—Elizabeth Bevarly
Crown and Glory
Shane Cordello was more than just strong muscles and a handsome face—he was also next in line for the throne of Penwyck. Then, as Shane and his escort, Sara Wallington, were en route to Penwyck, their plane was hijacked. And as the danger surrounding them escalated, so did their passion. But upon their return, could Sara transform the royal prince into a willing husband?

#1475 A Lawman in Her Stocking—Kathie DeNosky
Vowing not to have her heart broken again, Brenna Montgomery moved to Texas to start a new life—only to find her vow tested when her matchmaking grandmother introduced her to gorgeous Dylan Chandler. The handsome sheriff made her ache with desire, but could he also heal her battered heart?

#1476 Do You Take This Enemy?—Sara Orwig
Stallion Pass
When widowed rancher Gabriel Brant disregarded a generations-old family feud and proposed a marriage of convenience to beautiful—and pregnant—Ashley Ryder, he did so because it was an arrangement that would benefit both of them. But his lovely bride stirred his senses, and he soon found himself falling under her spell. Somehow Gabe had to show Ashley that he could love, honor and cherish her—forever!

SDCNM1002